Winds of Deception

Samantha Rite Series Book 2

Hope Callaghan

Visit my website for new releases and special offers: hopecallaghan.com

FIRST EDITION

hopecallaghan.com

Copyright © 2014
All rights reserved.

TABLE OF CONTENTS

"And the sea gave up the dead which were in it, and death and Hades gave up the dead which were in them; and they were judged, every one of them according to their deeds."
Revelation 20:13. KJV

Chapter 1

Sam's eyebrows scrunched together as she scowled at the phone, as if staring at it hard enough would make it disappear. She was never going to get the Collier quote done if the stupid phone didn't stop ringing! Her eyebrows furrowed as she growled at it in frustration. To say Sam was irritated would be an understatement. The 60 hour work-weeks were wearing on her. Instead of shrinking, the piles of paperwork just seemed to grow.

She ran a frazzled hand through her long dark hair. All this stress and aggravation was the direct result of her recent vacation. Admittedly, the cruise had been a welcome break but the mountain of work waiting for her when she got back left her wondering whether it was worth taking the time off.

Sam sighed heavily as she picked up the phone. "Thank you for calling Anderson Insurance Group. Samantha Rite speaking. How can I help you?"

"Samantha Rite, this is Special Agent James Donovan of the CIA." He got right to the point. "I need to meet with you as soon as possible."

Sam stared down at the phone in disbelief. "Why on earth do you need to meet with me?"

"We believe your life may be in danger," the caller responded.

This must be some kind of joke and it wasn't one bit funny. She had enough to worry about right now. "Sorry, I didn't catch that last part. Did you just say my life was in danger?"

The caller ignored her question. "I'm in town now and close to your office. I can meet you there or someplace else ... if you prefer." He paused for a second before he went on. "We need to meet today. The sooner the better."

He quickly continued before Sam could interrupt again. "Lee Windsor asked me to contact you. He's still in Central America and wasn't able to contact you himself. Since this is of utmost urgency, I agreed to come here and meet you."

Sam let out a mental sigh of relief. Well, at least Lee wasn't blowing her off. There had only been one short text from him since she got home. Last she knew, he was still in Belize and she was beginning to wonder …

She snapped back to the conversation at hand. "I'm not meeting you anywhere until you tell me what's going on."

Poor Lee, Donovan thought. *This lady sounded like a real handful. Maybe he just caught her at a bad time...*

Donovan repeated himself as he tried to stress the urgency in meeting, "Like I said before, there's a good chance your life may be in danger."

It looked as if Sam wasn't going to get any more information out of this Donovan fellow until she agreed to meet him. She mentally shrugged. It was probably best to err on the side of caution.

"OK, I'll meet you after I get out of work. There's a pub right around the corner from my office. But I can't make it until around 6," she warned.

As soon as she hung up, she texted Lee. *"I just got a call from a man who said he was Special Agent Donovan. He told me my life was in danger and he mentioned your name. Do you know what this is about?"* Sam hit send and then set her phone down. Hopefully, he would reply.

She spent the rest of the afternoon trying to focus on work but a thread of concern kept winding its way into her thoughts. *Was she really in danger?*

She worked hard to push the memories of her cruise back but they kept popping into her brain. She and her sister had planned a girls-only cruise – a 40th birthday celebration with a week spent in paradise. A much-needed escape after a really difficult year.

She let out a small sigh. Sam found out her husband had been cheating on her with a woman in his office – a much younger woman at that. It seemed like everyone in the world knew about it - except her. By the time the whole affair was out in the open, there was no chance of salvaging their marriage. Not that Anthony had tried – or even wanted to. The ink wasn't even dry on the divorce papers before the jerk married the "other woman."

The cruise hadn't exactly turned out as planned. Her sister had an accident and couldn't go so Sam ended up going by herself. Looking back, she was glad she went. Even if it did leave her with piles of work.

Everything had been going great until the day their ship made a final port stop in Belize. Her plan had been to go cave tubing up in the rainforest that day. Little did she know that their tour group would be taken hostage en route to the cave. After several harrowing hours, many of which Sam spent desperately praying, they were miraculously rescued by the U.S. military – and Lee.

Sam smiled as she thought about Lee. She was attracted to him from the moment she set eyes on him, even though he had been very standoffish, almost rude. It wasn't until the last day of her vacation she found out why. He was working undercover to track down wanted criminals - who just so happened to be the ones that abducted her and others during their excursion.

After it was over and they had all been rescued, Lee and Sam spent her last evening in the city getting to know each other. They discovered they had a lot in common and both had grown up in small Midwestern towns.

As the evening ended, they exchanged numbers and Lee assured her once he was back in the States he would give her a call. She had heard from him exactly once - a very brief text message, telling her he was wrapping things up and would call her soon. She was beginning to wonder if he really was interested, after all.

Until now. Somehow this must have something to do with the abduction in Belize. But what could anyone possibly want with her? The whole idea made her more than a little jittery.

Looking back, she wished she had just told this special agent to come to her office right then so she could get this over!

The hands on the clock seemed to stop as the rest of the afternoon dragged on. She kept glancing at her phone but Lee never replied.

Finally it was 5:30 and time to go meet this mysterious Special Agent Donovan. She grabbed her coat and purse and headed to the elevator. As she punched the down button, she looked at her watch for the umpteenth time as she tapped her foot on the floor. The elevator was taking forever!

When she finally reached the first floor, the doors slid silently open. Sam peeked around before stepping out. Although she couldn't see anyone, she had a nagging feeling that eyes were following her and she suddenly had a strong urge to start running. Instead, she strode across the lobby as fast as her high-heeled shoes would allow.

Once outside, she stopped to collect her thoughts, shaking her head as if to clear it. *I am so paranoid these days.* With a quick look around, she impulsively decided to take a shortcut through the adjacent parking garage, knowing it would get her to the meeting place faster. It would also give her a chance to drop her briefcase off in her car.

When she got to the edge of the garage, she suddenly realized just how dark it was inside. Dark and isolated. She stood still for a minute as she peered inside, giving her eyes time to adjust to the lack of light. Before she could change her mind and head back the way she had just come, she forced herself to start walking, making a quick beeline for her car.

She breathed a sigh of relief when she got to her car. She glanced down at the keys in her hand and for a second, was tempted to jump inside and drive off - forget about meeting this Donovan character.

Just then, she saw something move out of the corner of her eye. She narrowed her eyes as she looked in that direction but couldn't make anything out. A slight shiver ran down her spine. She was **certain** she had seen something move. She tossed her bag in the car and quickly locked it.

Sticking to the outer edge of the garage, Sam made her way towards the exit door as fast as her legs would take her, telling herself the entire time that there was nothing to be afraid of – there was nothing there.

Soon, she rounded the corner of the garage – the exit door was in sight. She let out a sigh of relief.

Just as she put her hand on the knob, someone stepped out from the shadows and grabbed her from behind. She felt a sudden jolt of fear as a wet rag was shoved into her face.

Sam turned and twisted as she frantically fought to free herself from the ironclad grip that was around her waist. The rag that covered her nose and mouth reeking of strong chemicals. Within seconds, a fog circled her brain. She tried to scream but no sound would come out. As she slipped into unconsciousness, Sam whispered a name …. *Lee*.

Chapter 2

Agent Donovan glanced nervously at his watch. It was now 6:45 and Samantha Rite was late. Donovan had a bad feeling.

He nervously wiped his brow as he dialed her office number. A recording of Samantha's chipper voice echoed back. Frustrated, Donovan shoved the phone in his pocket.

He began drumming his fingers on the gleaming bar top as he grabbed his drink and took a long swallow. Moments later, he pulled his cell phone back out. Time to try her cell again. The same happy voice answered back, "You have reached Sam's voice mail. I can't come to the phone right now. Please leave a message. Thanks and have a great day!"

Donovan leaned forward and stuck a fisted hand on his chin as he tried to think. *Maybe he should head over to her office, take a look around...*

The bartender glanced in his direction. It was still early and there were only a handful of people in the dimly lit watering hole. Joe was good at remembering faces and this guy wasn't a regular. "Everything OK, buddy?"

Donovan looked up as he slowly shook his head. "Let's just say I've had better days." You wouldn't describe Donovan as real tall. But what he lacked in height, he more than made up for in brawn. Years of cardio and weights kept him in tip-top shape. He loved to hit the boxing ring on his days off. It was a good way to blow off some of that pent up energy he always seemed to have from tracking down the bad guys.

He unconsciously ran a hand through his cropped hair. His intelligent green eyes stared intently at the neon clock on the wall and then shifted to the bar entrance, almost as if willing Samantha Rite to walk through. Those piercing eyes could bore into even the most hardened criminal and make him spill his guts.

But there was another side to Agent Donovan. When Donovan was in a good mood he would flash his famous smile. A smile that made the ladies swoon. Deep down, he was a real teddy bear and women adored him.

He'd had a few serious girlfriends over the years but none serious enough to make a long-term commitment. At almost 40 years old, he wasn't sure if he would ever find "the one."

Every once in a while, he felt a pang of loneliness when he watched happy families as they passed him on the street. It made him wonder if maybe – just maybe - he wasn't missing out, but deep down he knew he had never been ready. His favorite excuse was his work was too dangerous and he had to travel all the time. No sense in getting married just to leave a wife and kids at home.

James Donovan and Lee Windsor had been friends since grade school. They grew up in the same neighborhood, graduated from the same high school. They both joined the Navy at the same time. Lee went on to become a Navy Seal while Donovan decided on a career as a Special Agent with the CIA. The years had slipped by but their friendship was as strong as ever.

Donovan looked around, checked his phone one last time and finally stood up. This was not looking good. He hastily scribbled his cell phone number on a napkin and handed it to the bartender. "If a pretty, dark-haired brunette comes in and asks for Donovan, can you give her my number?"

The bartender picked up the napkin and glanced at the number as he shoved it in his shirt pocket. "Sure buddy. I hope she shows up for your sake." He patted his pocket. "If she does, I'll be sure to give her this."

Donovan sighed as he threw his jacket over his arm and headed towards the door. "Thanks and for my sake, I hope she shows up, too."

The sidewalk was almost empty and it was getting dark. Donovan glanced around. Judging from where he was at, he guessed it would only be about a 10 minute walk from her office to the bar - but which way would she go? There was a sidewalk out front - a direct path from her office here. His gaze focused on the parking garage – what if she decided to take a shortcut through there? His gut instinct told him she took the shortcut.

Donovan walked into the dimly lit garage and headed in the direction of her office on the opposite side. Always one for picking up even the smallest of details, he carefully looked around as he passed through. *Nothing suspicious here.* When he reached her building he wasn't surprised to find it was locked up tight.

Donovan glanced back towards the parking garage and let out an aggravated sigh. "Might as well get this over with," he mumbled under his breath.

Lee was furious. "What do you mean she never showed up??"

"I waited an hour past our meeting time and she never showed. I walked to her office but it was locked up tight. Place was dark." Donovan sighed. "I tried calling, texting. Pretty much blew up her phone and nothing."

The hair stood up on the back of Lee's neck. Even though he didn't know Sam that well, it sure didn't seem like something she would do. It wasn't like her to promise to meet someone and then not be there.

Lee started barking orders over the phone. "It's probably a waste of time, but I want you to run over to her house and see if anyone's around."

Donovan could hear the frustration in his voice as he went on, "I'm on my way up there now. My flight leaves in half an hour. Pick me up at the Grand Rapids Airport at 10:30 tonight."

Lee grimly continued, "Let's hope you have better news for me by the time I get there."

He hung up the phone and started pacing. He should've insisted on leaving Belize early and going to Michigan himself. It was his responsibility to protect Sam. After all, it was his fault she was involved in the first place. At least that's what he told himself.

A wave of anger filled Lee as he pounded his fist on the table in sheer frustration. He jerked his backpack out of the chair and stomped out of the room.

Chapter 3

Sam slowly tried lifting her head. It felt like a ton of bricks – a ton of bricks someone was pounding on with a sledge hammer. From far away, she thought she heard a car door slam. She was moving and the feeling of nausea was overwhelming, making her stomach churn. She swallowed hard, willing the gagging sensation to go away.

The fog finally began to lift and in a split second two realizations hit her. Her hands were tied behind her back and she was blindfolded. Fear spread over her entire body. She opened her mouth. For an irrational second, she thought about screaming but even in her foggy state, that didn't seem like a good idea so she quickly closed it. Something told her that would only make matters worse.

Her mind started to race. *Focus. Focus. OK, she was in a car and it was moving.* But how did she end up here and where was she going? Nothing was making sense.

The vehicle suddenly stopped and a door swung open. Cool evening air rushed in and enveloped her. There was no time to gather her bearings before strong arms grabbed her under her arms and dragged her from the seat. Whoever it was - was now carrying her.

With a few quick steps, she sensed they had stepped inside a building. Sam listened closely but the only sound she could hear was the abductor's footsteps echoing on a hard, cement floor. They must be in some kind of empty building, maybe a warehouse.

Sam nervously swallowed, her nausea threatening to come back with a vengeance. They took several more long strides before she was abruptly released. *"Oomph."* The sudden drop took her breath away. Thankfully, the fall was broken when she landed on some kind of cushion.

A silent prayer escaped her lips. *Please Heavenly Father. Protect me.* One of her favorite Bible verses came to mind.

Be strong and courageous. Do not be afraid or terrified because of them, for the Lord your God goes with you; he will never leave you nor forsake you. (Deuteronomy 31:6) **NIV**.

She drew a shaky, hiccupping breath. The air was hot and stifling. Wherever they were at – it smelled musty – like no one had been in there in a really long time.

Fear began to numb her mind. None of what was happening made any sense.

Maybe she could reason with whoever had brought her here. Sam swallowed hard as she tried to keep her voice from rising in panic. "Who are you? W-What do you want?" she stammered.

Sam lay there quietly, holding her breath as she waited for an answer. She could sense someone listening, could hear small movements but there was no response. "Listen, I'll give you whatever you want – just let me go."

Her voice dropped to a whimper. "No one will know who you are. Just tell me what you want..."

Even though she was blindfolded, Sam could sense she was being studied. A trickle of sweat, mixed with fear ran down her forehead.

Without warning, the abductor grabbed her ankles and shoved them together. Seconds later, a coarse, prickly rope was tied around them. She dug her fingernails into the palm of her hand. *Do not scream!*

That seemed to help a little but her mind was still racing. *I have no idea what this person wants with me. Why won't they just tell me what they want?*

She swallowed hard and licked her lips. "Please..." Before she could utter another word, a thick piece of duct tape was slapped across her mouth. Behind the blindfold, Sam's eyes widened in sheer panic as waves of terror washed over her.

Her heart was pounding out of her chest. *Oh no – not now!* The familiar feeling of claustrophobia pressed in on her.

Suddenly, the cushion shifted. Whoever had tied her up and taped her mouth had moved away. Footsteps echoed on the cement floor and then slowly faded. Seconds later she heard a door slam shut. Whoever it was had left her all alone.

Chapter 4

Lee's flight was right on time. Donovan was waiting for him in the terminal with a grim look on his face. Judging from his expression, there was no need for Donovan to confirm what Lee already knew.

"Nothing, huh?"

Donovan shook his head. "Not a trace. I ran a background on her, found her car in the parking garage. When I looked inside, I could see her briefcase so it appears she made it that far before vanishing into thin air."

He watched as Lee unconsciously clenched and unclenched the bag he was holding. He'd known him long enough to tell this was a sign of extreme agitation.

Donovan was filled with guilt. If only he had insisted on meeting Sam earlier at her office. Looking back, he should've just ignored her and shown up on her doorstep - forced her to listen to him.

Lee ran a hand through his short hair and took a deep breath as he glanced around the airport terminal. "Did you go by her townhouse yet?"

Donovan shook his head. "Nope. Figured we could do that once you got here."

"Well, let's get going." Lee pointed to his backpack. "Traveling light as usual. This is all I've got."

A short time later, Lee and Donovan pulled up in front of Sam's place. Not surprisingly, it looked deserted. The evening air was crisp and cool, the neighborhood quiet and peaceful except for a neighbor's dog barking in the distance.

They walked to the front entrance and rang the doorbell. After waiting a few minutes to see if anyone would answer, Lee dropped his backpack on the ground and began rummaging around inside.

When he pulled his hand back out, he was holding a long, slender pick. He expertly inserted the pick into the lock and after a couple quick jabs, it popped. Seconds later, the front door swung open.

Donovan grinned. "You always were one of the best in the business."

Lee smiled wryly. "Yeah, comes in handy every once in a while."

Lee stepped in first as he peered into the dark house. "Sam?" They waited. He called louder, "Sam, it's Lee. Are you home?" Nothing but eerie silence greeted them. It was obvious no one was there.

Lee reached out, groping the wall until his hand made contact with the light switch. Bright light instantly flooded the interior. The place was in shambles. Whoever was there before them left a huge mess. Closet doors had been flung wide open - all the contents dumped out on the floor below. Everything in the kitchen cabinets now lay on the counter, carelessly strewn from one end to the other. Kitchen drawers had been ripped out and tossed in a haphazard heap on the floor. Even the refrigerator was pulled away from the wall.

After surveying the mess in the kitchen, the two made their way into the living room where it wasn't much better. The floral-colored sofa had been destroyed and what was left of the cushions lay in a crooked pile in the middle of the floor where someone had taken a knife and shredded them.

Her brown leather recliner didn't look much better. There were chunks of padding everywhere.

Even the flat screen TV had been ruined. Whoever it was, had ripped the back off and pulled the wires out.

Lee shook his head as he surveyed the damage. "I'm almost afraid to look in the bedroom."

They weren't surprised to find that the same mess greeted them in there. The sheets had been yanked off the large four poster bed. The pillow top mattress looked like someone filled it with confetti and then dumped it out all over the room.

"Whoever did this has Sam." Lee looked soberly at Donovan. "I'm pretty sure I know who it is. Now we just have to find them."

He paused before continuing, "Let's go down to police headquarters. There's a packet of info waiting for me I'm hoping will help us figure out where they are."

With that, they retraced their steps to the front of the house, turning off the lights on the way out and carefully locking the door behind them.

Chapter 5

When Sam realized she was alone, she knew she needed to come up with an escape plan – and fast!

Think, Think!!

First things first. She had to figure out how to get the ropes off and since she wasn't able to see exactly how the knots were tied, she decided to start out by twisting her wrists away from each other. She bent her hands forward and stretched her fingers as far down as possible. *If only she could slip her fingernail under one of the outside knots.* She feverishly worked on the closest knot that was just within reach of her fingernail. The angle was all wrong and there was no way it was going to budge.

Sam's exhaustion and frustration turned to anger. Now was *not* the time to give up! She had to stay focused and get out of there!

Maybe she should try the ropes around her ankles. She started to wiggle her feet back and forth and found the rope giving a little. If she could bend far enough back she might be able to reach down and loosen the rope.

She took a deep breath and arched herself backward as far as she possibly could. Her neck was tilted at an odd angle as her face pointed upward.

It was hard to breathe with her mouth taped shut. Her heart began pounding at the thought of not having enough air. *Please God, do not let me have a panic attack now!*

Finally, her fingers latched onto the ropes. Her hands were sweating as she awkwardly fumbled with the ties. Her pulse raced as she easily untied the first three knots. Soon she would be free!

After the third knot was easily undone, her stomach plummeted when she discovered the rest of the knots were in the front!

I am NOT giving up! With a renewed sense of determination, she arched her back even further and at the same time tried to reach around to the front of her ankles.

It wasn't going to work. She just couldn't bend that far.

After taking a short, snorting breath through her nose, she cautiously moved her ankles back and forth. If she could loosen the ropes enough, maybe she could slip out of them...

She did this for several minutes and finally felt the rope give a little. The flesh on her ankles started to burn as the rough strands rubbed her skin raw. Sam pushed the pain aside and focused on freeing her legs and getting out of there before her abductor returned.

Just then, she heard a car pull up and a door slam. He was back! Seconds later, she heard the creak of a door as it was opened. Sam lay there quietly, praying he wouldn't notice what she'd been doing while he was gone.

The footsteps grew louder as her abductor drew near. She could feel eyes boring down on her. Suddenly, there was a firm grip on her ankles and the ropes were quickly tightened.

Sam was devastated, a wave of hopelessness and despair washed over her. She was so close to escaping!

She swallowed hard and began to pray. She knew that God was with her. Instantly she felt His presence and was filled with peace. She said a small prayer of thanksgiving. There was no way she could remain this calm without God.

The calm continued, even when she sensed a face, only inches from hers. She could feel a person's breath close by, as if she was being studied.

The cushion she was laying on shifted. Whoever it was - was now right beside her! Without warning, the duct tape was painfully ripped from her lips.

She gasped for air. Even though her face and lips were throbbing, she was relieved to have the tape off.

Sam jumped as a voice suddenly whispered in her ear, "Where is it? I need my papers back. What did you do with them?"

Finally, a voice. Instinctively, she had always known it was a male abductor judging by the arms that carried her and the heavy footsteps that echoed in the empty building.

But what on earth was he talking about? She didn't know anything about any "papers." Sam stammered, her words barely coherent as she forced herself to answer, "I, I d-don't know what you're talking about..."

The voice cut her off as the whisper turned to a shout, "I know you have them and I want them back – Now!"

Confused, Sam shook her head. Her voice wavered. "You have to believe me - I don't have your papers!"

Sam sensed the person abruptly moving away. The voice became muffled. Her abductor was talking but not to her.

"If I don't get them back soon, they're going to track me down and kill me. First, they'll kill you, then they'll kill me."

A horrifying thought entered her mind. *What if he brought someone back with him? What if there are TWO of them?*

But that voice. It was vaguely familiar. *Where had she heard that voice?*

She had no time to dwell on it. Her abductor stomped back over to where she was laying. She could feel hot breath on her cheeks. The voice was low and menacing. "We're going to go for a little ride to your place and you're going to show me where it is. If you don't, I'll be forced to drag it out of you. Slowly and painfully."

Sam's face froze, her heart pounding in her chest. She took a big gulp of air. "I … I d-don't know what you're looking for. Please, I have no idea..."

Her captor cut her off as he roughly shoved his hands under her arms and picked her up. In one motion, he tossed her over his shoulder and walked rapidly toward the door.

When they reached the outdoors, the cool night air hit Sam's face. She took a deep breath. It smelled a whole lot better out here than it did in that musty old building.

There was no time to enjoy what little bit of relief the fresh air could offer as a car door was flung open. Sam was carelessly shoved inside and the door quickly slammed shut. Her captor jumped in the car and moments later, they were on the road, headed to her house.

The ride to her place gave Sam some precious moments to think. She desperately tried to formulate a plan but the only thought swirling in her head was that she was about to die and she had no idea why.

The only thing she could hope for was a chance to stall him and figure out a way to escape. She was certain that even if he found what he was looking for, he was still going kill her.

A dizzying thought dawned on her. *If this person knows where I live, how long has he been stalking me?*

An image of Lee popped into her head. Obviously he had known something – but why didn't he just tell her? Why didn't Agent Donovan stress the danger she was in when he called?

Admittedly, Donovan tried to tell her that her life was in danger. She didn't completely blow it off but she obviously hadn't taken it as seriously as she should have.

A glimmer of hope filled Sam. Surely Donovan and Lee would be looking for her by now since she never showed up to meet Donovan. What if they're there waiting for me at my house? Sam lay motionless as she contemplated a possible rescue.

"Please Dear God," Sam prayed. *"Please save me. I don't want to die..."*

It seemed like they were riding forever before the car finally stopped. The passenger door opened. Sam was roughly yanked out of the back seat and half-carried, half-dragged to her doorstep.

Her abductor kept one arm around her, holding her in a tight grip while the other was rattling a set of keys. Her mouth went dry, her mind reeling when she realized he had *her* keys. The keys to her house. That meant he must have her purse, too. Until that moment, she hadn't even thought about her purse.

Seconds later, the door opened and she was dragged inside. One of her high-heeled shoes slipped off as it caught on the door frame. The shoe went unnoticed as the door was quickly slammed shut.

Her abductor set her down, his voice whispered menacingly in her ear. "Home Sweet Home. Now you better think **real hard** about what you did with my papers."

Sam was left balancing precariously on uneven feet, her ankles still tied together. For a split second, she had the urge to scream as loud as she could at the top of her lungs in the hopes that there was the teensiest chance her neighbor might hear.

Any thought of that was quickly forgotten as a cold piece of metal was pressed against the side of her face – a gun!

The menacing voice continued. "I'm going to untie you and take off your blindfold but if you scream or raise your voice even just a little, I'm going to blow your head off, you got that?"

Sam swallowed hard and nodded her head, too terrified to even whisper a reply.

With that, her abductor untied her feet first. Pain from the rope burns seared Sam's skin but there was no time to dwell on it.

After her legs were freed, the ropes on her wrists were loosened and then yanked off.

The blindfold was the last thing to go. She blinked her eyes rapidly as they tried to adjust. The room was dark – almost pitch black and Sam had trouble focusing. As her eyes finally began registering her surroundings, they moved to the living room window. There was no light streaming in, so it must be the middle of the night.

Without warning, the hallway light was switched on and Sam was temporarily blinded. She reached out to grab the wall and steady herself, blinking several times until her eyes began to focus for a second time.

When she was able to look around, she almost wished he had left the blindfold on. Her heart sunk. Her home was in absolute shambles, almost completely destroyed.

Sam closed her eyes, trying to wrap her mind around this unbelievable, nightmarish situation. She opened them again and choked back a sob. Not one single thing in her home was in its place. Everything had either been upended or completely destroyed.

There was only one place left to look. Her gaze slowly and fearfully turned to the man standing nearby. As her eyes traveled upwards, she could see that her abductor was lean and tall and was wearing a dark jacket with black slacks.

She slowly lifted her gaze. His face was covered with a black ski mask. The only thing visible were two beady little eyes that peered out at her from small, round holes.

When he saw she was starting at him, he leaned forward and spoke. "Now go get the papers!"

Sam turned ashen-colored as the blood drained from her face. "I told you, I d-don't know what you're talking about."

Sam looked at her captor with pleading eyes. "I swear, I don't know what you're looking for." She looked around. "Don't you think if I had it, you would've found it by now? You destroyed my home!"

That answer only seemed to enrage him as he grabbed her arm and half-shoved, half-dragged her into the living room. When they got there, he pushed her towards the center of the room and pointed the gun directly at her. "You have one minute to tell me where it is or I'm going to kill you!"

Chapter 6

Inside the station, Lee and Donovan quickly scanned the packet of papers spread out on the table. It didn't take long before Lee leaned back in his chair, a thoughtful expression on his face. "Just what I thought."

He tossed the picture he was holding across the table in Donovan's direction. "We've been tracking him for some time now. This is the person who has Sam."

Donovan glanced at the picture before he opened his mouth to say something. Just then, his cell phone rang and he quickly answered it.

Lee watched Donovan's expression as it grew serious. "Yes. Yes, that's awesome! Give me the address. We'll head over there now."

Donovan quickly scribbled something on a piece of paper and handed it to Lee. "This is where they're at – Sam and the guy you've been looking for."

Lee glanced at the piece of paper Donovan had just written on. It was an address he knew all too well.

He jumped out of his char. "We've got to go now! This guy is ruthless. If he doesn't get what he wants – Sam's a goner!"

On their way to the car, Lee turned to Donovan. "How'd they get that address so fast?"

Donovan grinned like a Cheshire Cat. "We've had surveillance on this guy for a while now. We got a lucky break not too long ago when he left his cell phone in his car. We had just enough time to stick a tracer on it before he came back to get it. We've been tracking him ever since."

He continued, "When you told me who it was, I sent a message to the department so they could pinpoint his exact location."

Lee's expression grew grim. "I just hope we make it in time. This guy is a real nut job. Who knows what he'll do if he doesn't get what he wants."

The drive to Sam's house seemed to take forever. Visions of Sam's lifeless body sprawled out on the floor made Lee want to break every speed limit there was.

When they finally pulled into her neighborhood, they parked the car a short distance away and made the rest of the trip on foot.

Finally, her townhome was in view. There was a car in the driveway and it wasn't hers.

Since walking up to the front door and ringing the bell wasn't an option, they threw together a hasty plan to head to the back of the house and look in the windows.

As they made their way to the back, Donovan glanced around. His sharp eye spied something lying on the front step. They crept over to take a closer look. It was a shoe! A woman's high-heeled shoe was dangling on the porch stoop. Sam was in the house!

It was too early to celebrate but it gave them hope she was there and that they had reached her in time.

The two picked up the pace as they tiptoed past and headed to a side window first. Lee slowly lifted his head as he tried to glimpse inside. The shades were drawn and there were no holes or gaps to peek through. Lee shook his head in Donovan's direction.

Donovan slowly inched his way to the corner of the house and cautiously peered into the living room slider. He looked at Lee and shook his head as he whispered, "closed tight."

Lee jerked his head back towards the last window. It was Sam's bedroom and they could see a bright light pouring out. Finally, a window without shades! They cautiously looked inside but no one was around.

"They must be in the living room or kitchen," Lee whispered.

Donovan motioned to Lee. As they moved a short distance away and out of earshot, he began talking. "We're going to have to just bust our way into the house and take our chances."

"I'm sure he has a weapon – probably a gun - so the only chance we have is the element of surprise," he reasoned.

Donovan patted his hip. "I have my Glock, but I'm guessing you don't want to use this unless absolutely necessary."

Lee nodded. "I don't want to chance Sam getting caught in the crossfire."

Donovan stared at the ground. "We need a better plan." He looked around. "What if one of us busts through the front while the other one smashes through the dining room window?"

Lee was skeptical. The plan was shaky at best. "You don't think there's a chance the garage side door is unlocked ...?"

Donovan shrugged. He hadn't thought of that. It was worth a shot.

They quietly made their way over to the garage door and Lee slowly turned the knob. He shook his head. "It's locked."

Donovan glanced at the door frame before reaching up and slowly running his hand over the top of the frame. "Bingo!" He pulled his hand back down and in it was a key.

Within seconds the door was unlocked and they silently slipped inside. The room was pitch black so it took a few seconds for their eyes to adjust.

Finally, they could see enough to know the garage was empty.

There was no time to look around. They cautiously made their way toward the door leading into the kitchen.

Lee reached out to turn the door knob. It was locked. He took a step back and with as much force as possible, he kicked the door wide open...

Chapter 7

A nagging sense of foreboding inched its way up Sam's spine as she carefully maneuvered through the piles of what used to be her life but was now nothing more than a heartbreaking mound of trash on her floor.

Not only was she was filled with thoughts of her impending doom, she started to get angry. REALLY angry! She had done nothing to deserve being kidnapped, terrorized and have her home destroyed.   She took several deep breaths as she fought to control the rage that was beginning to consume her.

She didn't need to turn around to know that a set of sharp, cruel eyes were closely following her.

Desperate to buy some time, she slowly walked around the room, occasionally bending down to pick something up.

The gunman grew impatient when he realized she was stalling. He angrily strode towards her as he shouted, "get it and get it now!"

She pretended not to hear him as she worked to quiet her inner rage. She tightly clenched her fists as she slowly turned to face him, her expression unreadable.

With every ounce of self-control she could summon, she haltingly replied, "I **told** you, I don't…"

Just then, she was interrupted by a loud commotion coming from the kitchen. It sounded as if someone had just come crashing through her garage door.

Her abductor gave Sam a warning look as if to say, "stay put." With that, he turned on his heel and ran to the kitchen doorway.

Sam stared at his retreating back, fury still raging inside of her. Now was her only chance to save herself!

Her eyes quickly darted around the room and finally settled on a heavy brass lamp that was lying on the floor near her feet. It was one her grandmother had given her before she died. At the thought of that and all the precious things this worthless loser carelessly destroyed, Sam was once again filled with a seething anger that threatened to boil over.

From where she stood, she could see him in the hallway as he peeked around the corner that led out to the kitchen. It was time to make her move!

Sam reached down and grabbed the heavy lamp off the floor. She quietly crept up behind her abductor.

Using both hands, she lifted the lamp high above her head and with as much force as she could muster, she slammed the lamp down on the back of the masked man's skull. He staggered backwards, grabbing his head as he reeled around to face Sam.

At that exact moment, two shadowy figures barreled out of the kitchen and into the hallway. Like a steamroller, they tackled Sam's abductor and shoved him to the ground.

The three of them began rolling around on the floor as one of them struggled to grab the gun that was tightly clenched in the gunman's hand.

There was no time to think! Sam rushed over to the pile of thrashing arms and legs as all three men fought to gain control.

She carefully watched as each of them wrestled back and forth.   Finally, Sam saw her opportunity to make a move. All her anger was now focused on her tormentor and with all the anger spilling out at that exact moment, she stomped on the gunman's hand with the tip of her only remaining high-heeled shoe.

The second her sharp heel made contact with his flesh, she ground her foot back and forth, determined to leave her mark. The gunman shrieked in pain as he loosened his grip on the weapon.

Sam quickly jumped out of the way.

Seizing the opportunity to finally grab the gun, one of the intruders snatched it from his loosened grip and freed himself from the scuffle still being played out on the floor.

He quickly jumped to his feet as he leveled the gun at Sam's tormenter. "Freeze!"

The fighting stopped instantly as both men lay motionless on the ground.

Seconds later, the second man crawled away from Sam's abductor and pulled himself to his feet.

He stood there for a long moment as he struggled to catch his breath.

When he finally turned around, his eyes met Sam's. Her jaw dropped and all the color drained from her face as she whispered, "Lee."

By the time Sam was able to suck in a deep breath, Lee was beside her. In one motion, he wrapped his arms around her shaking shoulders.

All her pent up emotions spilled over as she buried her head in his chest and began to sob uncontrollably.

Donovan couldn't stand the thought of a crying woman as he shifted uncomfortably from one foot to the other. In fact, it made him really, really mad!

With that thought in mind, he looked down at the scowling masked man and did the one thing that was going to give him *GREAT* pleasure.

Donovan pulled a set of handcuffs from his pants pocket and with considerable enthusiasm, snapped them on the thug.

"OUCH!!"

He looked down at the creep's beady little eyes with disgust. "Ooh, what's the matter? Cuffs a little too tight?"

After making sure his captive wasn't going anywhere, Donovan pulled out his phone and called for back-up.

He looked over to where Lee and Sam were still standing. "Ten minutes and they'll be here to pick up our friend."

Sam pulled away from Lee's embrace as she wiped the last of her tears with the back of her hand. Her sad, upturned face gazing into his.

"I'm sorry...I-I couldn't stop the meltdown." She attempted a half-hearted smile.

Lee reached out and caressed her cheek. "You have every right. In fact, I'd have to wonder what was wrong with you if there weren't any tears."

He grabbed her hand and gave it a reassuring squeeze, then turned to look at Sam's tormentor.

It was a good thing she couldn't see the look on Lee's face when he turned away, but Donovan recognized it and quickly took a step back.

48

Lee angrily strode over to the cuffed, masked man. He bent down, his face mere inches from the man reclining against the wall. In one swift motion, he reached over and grabbed a fistful of black ski mask mixed with hair.

He turned back to where Sam was still standing. "Time to put a face on the coward that destroyed your home and had every intention of killing you." He didn't wait for an answer before he yanked off the mask.

Sam gasped as she stared at her abductor. Somehow, he looked different than she remembered. He'd always given her an odd feeling but looking at him now, he seemed downright sinister. She shook her head in disbelief.

Michel jerked away from Lee as he looked back at Sam and sneered. "If not for your boyfriend, I would have been long gone by now."

He turned to glare at Lee. "You got me but there are others – and they'll be looking for the map. Just don't expect them to be as nice as I was."

Moments later, Donovan led two uniformed police officers into Sam's house.

"I think we've heard enough." Lee grabbed Michel's arm and roughly jerked him to his feet. "Looks like your ride is here. I'll see you in a little while and then you and I are going to have a nice long chat." With that, the police led Michel away.

After the three disappeared out the door, Lee turned to Sam. "You haven't officially met Donovan. Special Agent James Donovan, this is Samantha Rite."

Donovan stepped forward, a sheepish look on his face. "I owe you an apology..."

Sam held up her hand to stop him as she shook her head. "You're not to blame. It was my own stupid fault. You tried to tell me and I was just being stubborn. Looks like I got what I deserved..."

Lee cut in. "There's no way you deserved to be kidnapped and have your home ruined. It was my fault. I should've called you myself."

Sam looked at Donovan solemnly as she put her hand on his arm. "Thank you for trying to keep me from harm."

She looked over at Lee. "I just have to say...when Michel had me blindfolded, I thought the voice sounded vaguely familiar but it just dawned on me...he didn't have that French accent anymore. So that was fake?"

Donovan and Lee nodded in unison. "Yeah, there was nothing genuine about that guy. Everything he ever told you was a big, fat lie."

More questions kept popping into her head. "So what's this map Michel is looking for? He kept saying I had something that was his. But he kept calling them papers."

Lee started to explain, "he obviously didn't want to tell you what it was in case you really didn't know."

"You're not going to believe this but he's looking for a map – a treasure map that's worth a whole lot of money."

Sam's eyes widened in disbelief as she looked at Lee and then over at Donovan.

Lee took a deep breath. "Maybe I should go back and start at the beginning."

"There's a Spanish ship, the San Miguel that sunk off the coast of Florida back in 1715. In fact, the last sighting of it was just north of St. Augustine, Florida."

"It got caught in a fierce hurricane that destroyed its sails and navigation system. For hours, it was tossed around like a cork in the ocean until it eventually sank. At the time it went down, it was full of treasure, headed home to Spain."

"Everyone onboard went down with it. Everyone that is, except for one person who managed to make it to shore alive. It was the ship's captain. He died shortly after washing up on the beach but not before he drew a crude map of where the ship sunk. The map was found near his dead body," Lee explained.

"For almost 300 years now, the ship and its treasure have been laying at the bottom of the ocean. Only a few rare coins have ever been recovered."

He paused for a moment before going on. "The map went missing decades ago and rumors are flying that it finally surfaced and was being sold on the black market – for millions of dollars."

Lee looked at Sam. "That's where Michel comes in. He was paid handsomely by someone in the States to smuggle the map onto a cruise ship – our cruise ship – to buyers in Mexico."

"From what we can gather, Michel didn't know exactly what he was smuggling into Mexico until after he picked it up. But until we get a chance to interrogate him, we can only speculate. What that has to do with you remains to be seen."

He continued, "when we got to Belize, the CIA was hot on the trail of the map – and Michel. But they wanted to flush out the rest of the bad guys – whoever Michel was to rendezvous with."

"That's where I came in. Authorities knew something was going down on that trip but they didn't know exactly what until after the ship set sail from Miami. By the time they figured out the exchange was to happen first in Mexico and later, Belize, they made the decision to let it play out in the jungle."

Lee patted Sam's back. "I know it was scary but the good guys were close by at all times. They just had to wait until the right moment to pounce – to make sure everyone was safe. So they waited until it was dark and everyone was safely in their tents. Plus, they had night vision goggles and the abductors didn't. They wanted to take every advantage possible."

Donovan finished the story. "The abductors apparently moved Michel to another location before the camp was raided. After they found out he had hidden the map, they let him go with a warning. If he didn't hand over the map in seven days, they would kill him. A slow, painful and torturous death."

"So he's pretty desperate to get his hands on the map..." Lee added.

Sam's lips started to quiver and her eyes filled with tears as she looked around. "Well, it's not like he hasn't tried..."

Lee put an arm around Sam's shoulders. "Sam, I am so sorry. It seems every time you're with me you're either being stalked, getting kidnapped and now your home has been destroyed."

Sam choked back a sob. The stress of the last 24 hours was taking its toll. "Yeah, maybe I shouldn't hang out with you anymore!"

Lee cupped her chin in his hand as he gazed into her tear-filled eyes. "We will have all this replaced and repaired – it'll be like brand-new. I promise. But there's nothing we can do about it right now," he reasoned. "Why don't you go grab some things and we'll spend the night at a nearby hotel?"

He looked around in disgust at the damage Michel had caused. "We can worry about this tomorrow."

The three of them grabbed a quick bite to eat on their way to the hotel. At the elevator, Sam and Lee told Donovan good-night with the men agreeing to ride down to the station together in the morning to question Michel.

Lee walked Sam to her room and when they reached her door, he apologized again. "I'm so sorry you got dragged into this, Sam." He paused as he looked down at her tired, sad face. "But if you hadn't been caught in the middle, I never would've met you..."

Sam swallowed hard as she forced a smile. "Well, I GUESS you're worth a little trouble," she joked.

His look got serious when their eyes met. He leaned his head towards her and then slowly lowered his lips. Sam had never noticed the small scar on the edge of Lee's brow. For a brief moment, she wondered how he got it.

Sam closed her eyes, desperately wanting to feel his lips on hers. At first, his kiss was soft and gentle, almost as if it was a question. She leaned into him, her arms resting on his broad chest where she could feel his heart pounding.

It didn't take long before the kiss turned from a question to a demand. Demanding more attention, more response as his lips explored hers. A sea of emotions threatened to swallow her up.

Tearing his lips away from her mouth, they made a slow path across her cheek and down the curve of her neck, leaving a trail of hot spots in their wake.

Sam reached up to put her hands around Lee's neck as she pulled him even closer to her. The trailing kisses ended when Lee buried his face in her hair, breathing her in.

By the time Lee finally pulled away, Sam was breathing unsteadily. He looked down at her, his eyes dark and unreadable. "I'm not sorry, either."

Sam paused for a minute as she thought about what he just said and then laughed. "Well, I'm glad!"

As much as she would have thoroughly enjoyed another kiss that made her insides melt, she sighed and said, "I guess we better call it a day."

Lee nodded in agreement. "I'll be at the station first thing in the morning to start questioning Michel." He continued, "We'll be turning in a report on the damage to your place so you'll be reimbursed. I hope he didn't destroy anything that can't be replaced."

A small frown formed on Sam's brow. "I hope not, either." She sighed again as she shook her head. "We'll find out soon enough."

Lee glanced at this watch. "As soon as I'm done with him tomorrow, I'll give you a call and let you know what we find out."

With that, he gave her a tender good-night hug and then he was gone.

Chapter 8

Brianna let out an exasperated sigh. "We lost the car – *again*!" She and Jasmine had been wandering aimlessly around the massive theme park parking lot for over an hour.

By now, Brianna was more than just a little perturbed when she suddenly stopped and put her hands on her hips. "I am *positive* we parked in the Pixie Dust lot!"

Jasmine shook her head as she vehemently disagreed with her friend. "No, I'm almost 100% certain we parked in the Wooly Mammoth section."

The two girls were best friends since second grade – and complete opposites in every way. Jasmine was outgoing and impulsive where Brianna was more reserved and thoughtful. Brianna was wavy blonde hair and big blue-eyes while Jasmine had long, straight brown hair and deep, golden-brown eyes.

Brianna let out a loud, exaggerated breath as she whipped her cell phone out of her back pocket. Deader than a doornail. She looked at Jasmine and then down at the cell phone in Jasmine's hand. She shook her head. "Mine's dead, too."

"Ugh!!" Brianna stomped her foot in frustration. "Couldn't at least *one* of us thought to charge our phone?"

Before she could answer, a golf cart rounded the corner and pulled up beside them. A handsome, dark-haired security guard leaned forward, his arms coming to rest on the steering wheel. "You two look lost. Let me guess – you can't find your car!"

Jasmine eyes filled with tears she was so relieved to see security. "We have no idea where we parked." She held up her phone. "On top of that - our phones are dead!"

He smiled. "Happens all the time. That's why I'm here – to help beautiful damsels in distress track down their vehicles."

With that, he waved a hand at the back seat. "Hop in and we'll go find your chariot."

The girls were downright giddy. He didn't need to ask them twice! Before he had a chance to change his mind, they hopped in the back seat of the cart.

He opened his mouth to say something but was stopped when the girls started arguing again about where they thought the car was parked. He shook his head. There was no way he was getting in the middle of that argument.

Without saying a word, he stomped on the pedal and headed in the direction of the Pixie Dust lot.

Minutes later, they were circling the enormous, concrete layers. He glanced back in his mirror. "Start pressing your car alarm so we can figure out if it's in this area."

Bri and Jasmine stopped arguing for a moment as they stared at each other. "Why didn't *we* think of that??"

It wasn't long before they heard the alarm go off nearby. Seconds later, their car was in sight.

When the golf cart stopped, Jasmine turned to their handsome rescuer, a huge smile lighting up her face. "We definitely owe you one." She paused.

"Hey! We're staying at a hotel not far from here. "Maybe we can meet you later – after you get off work and buy you a drink? You know, kind of pay you back for helping us out..."

The young security guard looked at her thoughtfully. "Well, normally I would say no..."

Jasmine's face fell. She was really hoping he would say yes.

He continued. "But I guess I can make an exception. Just this once. But I don't get off until 10," he added.

Brianna quickly spoke up. "Oh, that's not a problem."

He looked thoughtfully from one girl to the other. Finally, he nodded. "OK. By the way – I'm Luke."

Jasmine spoke first as she pointed to herself. "I'm Jasmine and this is my friend Brianna." Then, before he could change his mind she quickly added, "So where do you want to meet?"

"There's a little pub, The Yellow Jacket, just down the road on International Drive. I can meet you there around 10:30?"

The girls nodded in unison. As they turned to get in the car, Brianna blurted out, "And you can bring a friend...if you want." Jasmine turned to her friend, her eyebrows raised. Brianna blushed as she looked at the ground.

Luke didn't seem to notice. "Sounds good. I'll find out if my buddy, Travis, can come. He's an Orange County EMT. We were supposed to meet up later after I got out of work tonight anyways..." he trailed off.

Jasmine nervously tugged on a long strand of hair. "Yeah, that would be great. We just got here last night so we haven't really done anything fun yet... except get lost in your parking lot."

Luke laughed. "Well, I'm glad you did." He reached down and started the cart. "I better get back to work. See you around 10:30 then."

After they were inside the car with the door firmly shut, Brianna turned to Jasmine, "I hope his friend is HALF as cute as he is." It was turning out to be a great first day of their vacation!

They arrived back at the hotel a short time later. The hotel was nice enough. It wasn't a five-star luxurious resort but the girls thought it was perfect. Mainly because it was right in the middle of all the action. Tons of little shops, restaurants, mini-golf, some tourist attractions, all within walking distance.

As they walked through the hotel lobby, they spied a young couple they recognized from the night before. All four of them had checked in at the same time.

Just as they passed by, the woman abruptly stopped. "Hey, I remember you from check-in last night. Have you guys ever been here before?"

Brianna shook her head. "No, this is our first time. We're not too familiar with the area," she confessed. "But I'm pretty sure the front desk can help you out..." Her voice trailed off.

The dark haired lady continued. "We were trying to figure out where to have dinner. You know, not super-expensive and within walking distance.

The traffic is crazy so we figured the less driving we have to do, the better."

Jasmine spoke up. "Someone told us about a restaurant a couple doors down – Mexican Masterpiece. I don't think it's very cheap, though. We were thinking of trying it ourselves."

The man quickly interjected, "Do you mind if we join you? Err, unless..."

The girls glanced at each other. Brianna shrugged. "Sure, we were going to walk over there around 8-ish."

Taking that as an invitation, the woman turned to Brianna, "That sounds like fun! By the way, my name is Vivian and this is my husband, Jimmy."

"I'm Brianna and this is my friend, Jasmine."

They all agreed to meet in the lobby a little while later. With that, the girls waved good-bye to their new friends and headed up to their room.

After the elevator door closed, Bri turned to Jasmine. "How did that happen? We don't even know these people. Don't you think that was kind of weird?" she added.

Jasmine nodded, "Yeah, it *did* seem a little odd - but it's not like we're riding anywhere with them. We should be pretty safe just going around the corner, right?"

By the time they made their way to the Mexican restaurant, it was "hoppin'." The restaurant was just what they expected - touristy and expensive.

They were quickly seated and the waitress came by for their drink order. After a few minutes of talking, the girls discovered Jimmy and Vivian were from California.

Brianna's face lit up. "I've been thinking of moving to either California or down to this area. Is California as expensive as they say?"

Jimmy answered first. "Unless you have a really good job and make lots of money, renting an apartment in a safe area is really expensive. Of course, it depends on what part of California..."

"I was thinking maybe San Diego?"

Vivian agreed. "Yeah, you need lots of money to live in a decent neighborhood. I've heard Florida's a lot cheaper than Cali."

66

Bri looked thoughtful. "Yeah, that's kind of what I thought..." she trailed off.

The food finally arrived and the waitress set huge plates of tacos, enchiladas and burritos in front of the girls. Jasmine's eyes widened. "No way can we eat all of this. The hotel room has a fridge, right?"

After they finished eating and the plates were cleared, Bri looked at her watch. It was 10 p.m. She glanced at Jasmine and then looked over at Jimmy and Vivian. "I'm sorry but we have to go. We're meeting some friends at a nearby pub. Maybe we can get together again before you leave?" she offered.

Vivian nodded. "That would be great." She quickly added, "What are you guys doing tomorrow?"

Jasmine spoke up. "We're not really sure yet. Why don't you give me your cell number and we'll call or text you once we've had a chance to talk about it."

Jimmy stood up and stretched. "Sounds good." He changed the subject. "We went to Empire Studios today..."

Brianna cut in. "Wow, that's where we were at! It was a blast but a little hot... and we lost our car in the parking lot..."

Vivian and Jimmy laughed. "Not hard to do at that place!"

"We were thinking maybe a water park or spending the day at Planet Earth tomorrow." Vivian continued, "We want to go to the beach, too. I heard Cocoa Beach isn't too far away."

A look of surprise crossed Brianna's face. "Sounds a lot like our plans."

Before Jimmy and Vivian could invite themselves again, she quickly added, "We'll talk about it and get back with you guys."

They waved good-bye to their new friends and headed in the opposite direction of the hotel.

After they were out of earshot, Bri whispered to Jasmine. "I hate to say this, but don't you think there are a whole lot of odd coincidences - either having done the same things or planning to do the same things we're going to do?"

Jasmine agreed. "It's creeping me out just a little - but they seem nice enough…"

Brianna's voice of reason kicked in. "I'm not saying completely avoid them but we need to be cautious. They are, after all, complete strangers."

There was no more time to discuss it. They had reached the pub and it was 10:30 on the dot.

They stepped inside and looked around. The place was packed but not so packed that the girls weren't able to spot Luke. He saw them at the exact same moment and waved them over.

As they started walking towards him, Bri glanced over at the guy sitting next to Luke. She let out a huge sigh of relief. *Awesome! He was as cute – if not cuter - than Luke.*

She smiled at Jasmine as she whispered under her breath, "Sure am glad we misplaced that car!"

They all hit it off instantly. Bri and Jasmine discovered that Travis was not only an EMT, he was a part-time firefighter. Brianna quickly decided he was one of the most interesting men she had met in years!

Jasmine was just as enchanted with Luke. She found out he was working his way through medical school and starting his residency in the radiology field that fall. Jasmine almost fainted when she found out. Hot guy, smart and on his way to becoming a doctor!

Briana wasted no time explaining to Travis and Luke that she was in Florida scoping out the area and she planned to move down with her mom now that she had finished college.

Travis grinned. "I'll be happy to show you around, give you some pointers on where to live, tell you what companies are hiring."

Jasmine glanced at Luke and added, "Yeah, I'm thinking about moving down here, too."

Bri's head swung around, her eyebrows raised as she stared at Jasmine. "So you were waiting to surprise me with that news? That's the first I've heard of this!"

Jasmine flashed Bri a sly smile. "I'm beginning to like Orlando more by the minute!"

The evening flew by. Finally, it was time to go. Luke turned to Jasmine, "So what are you plans for tomorrow?"

Bri looked hesitantly at Jasmine and answered. "We haven't really decided yet. It's either the beach or another theme park." She shrugged uncertainly, "I guess it depends on the weather."

Travis sounded excited. "We'd love to take you to the beach!" He waved his hand in Luke's direction. "We both have tomorrow off.   Cocoa is awesome and I think the weather is going to be perfect."

The girls glanced at each other warily. Brianna's mother would *not* be happy if she found out they got into a car with two guys they barely knew. "We'd like that a lot. If you don't mind, maybe we can we just follow you in our car?"

Travis instantly realized the reason for their hesitation. "Yes! Absolutely! You can just follow us there."

With that, they let out a sigh of relief and excitedly nodded their heads in unison. They agreed to meet the next morning in the hotel lobby and then parted ways for the evening.

On the walk back to the hotel, the girls were almost beside themselves. Chattering away at how awesome these guys were and how lucky they were that they lost the car.

Just as they reached the hotel, they remembered Jimmy and Vivian. Bri looked at her watch. "It's late. Let's just text them and tell them we can't meet them tomorrow but maybe another day..." Her voice trailed off.

Since it was late, Bri texted her Mom to let her know they were safely in the hotel for the night and they were going to the beach the next day. She didn't mention Travis or Luke. No sense in sending up red flags just yet.

Brianna's mom had become obsessively overprotective with her since her vacation. Her mom briefly mentioned some sort of incident that took place during one of the excursions but Brianna didn't know about the kidnapping or that three of the people from the tour group had been taken and were still missing.

Ever since she came back from the trip, she was constantly calling Brianna, making her check-in and she'd never done that before.

Chapter 9

Sam woke early the next morning. She spent most of the night tossing and turning, worrying about her house and what there was left to salvage.

She grabbed her phone off the nightstand and looked at the screen. Brianna had sent her a text late last night letting her know she and Jasmine were both safe and having a great time so far.

Sam let out a sigh of relief as she texted her back and told her she loved her. She purposely avoided mentioning Michel and being kidnapped. After all, it was over now and she'd just as soon put it behind her.

She had a second text. This one was from Lee. *I'm sorry again, for the mess Michel made of your house. Sending someone by around 10 a.m. to help you clean up. See you soon. Love, Lee.*

Sam was touched by Lee's concern. A small smile lit up her face. *He really was a great guy.*

She quickly got dressed and ran downstairs to grab a taxi since her car was still at work. A short time later she was standing inside her hallway staring around in disbelief. It was worse than she remembered from the night before.

From the looks of the place, there wasn't one single thing left untouched. Everything that hadn't been torn apart or dumped on the floor was destroyed.

It was just too much! She put her head in her hands as tears threatened to spill over. Before she could have a complete meltdown right there in the hallway, her doorbell rang.

She grabbed a Kleenex and quickly wiped away her tears, took a deep breath and swung open the front door. Standing in front of her were two big, burly guys in police uniform with solemn faces. Beside them was a petite, smiling, gray-haired lady.

The woman spoke first. "Hello my dear. Lee Windsor sent us over. Heard you had a big mess to clean up. Some moron did a number on your place and we're here to get it back in ship-shape condition."

Sam offered a shaky smile. She immediately liked the woman's no-nonsense attitude. It reminded her of a drill sergeant.

The woman could see Sam was visibly upset and quickly continued. "I'm Lieutenant Barcheski but you can call me Andrea. And these are Officers Jensen and Conrad. But you can call them whatever you want!"

The tone of her voice brought a small smile to Sam's lips. This lady was a real trip!

She opened the door wide as she let them inside.

Andrea immediately put the two burly officers to work in the kitchen. They brought a clipboard with them and meticulously wrote down everything that was broken or needed to be repaired. Thankfully, the kitchen looked worse than it really was. There were only a few small broken dishes and glasses – none of which held any sentimental value.

Andrea and Sam left Jensen and Conrad in the kitchen as they made their way to the bedroom in the back of the house.

When she got there, Sam paused in the doorway for a moment. She slowly made her way over to the closet door and peered inside. She was scared to look too closely. This is where she stored

her meticulously cared-for, priceless treasures –
heirlooms her Grandmother passed down to her
before her death last year. She also had several boxes
of irreplaceable drawings, crayon-colored cards, and
handmade presents lovingly crafted by daughter,
Brianna, when she was little girl.

She breathed a sigh of relief as she carefully
sifted through the piles. Only a couple of the small
gifts Brianna made for her were damaged beyond
repair. Everything else was in good shape.

By noon, they had made good progress and
Sam's stomach began to growl. *How rude of me. I
should be asking them if they would like to take a
break and have some lunch.* She left Andrea in the
bedroom and made her way to the kitchen.

As she rounded the corner, she heard a loud
noise. "Burrrippp!!!!!"

Sam stopped dead in her tracks. Seconds
later, "what was **that**?"

"Uhmm... I don't know."

Suddenly there was laughter. "Dude, you
ripped your drawers!"

"Really?? What the heck??? Oh no!!!!!"

Sam couldn't take it anymore. She had to see what on earth the two of them were doing in there. As she stepped over the threshold, she could see Conrad holding the seat of his pants while Jensen was doubled-over, laughing hysterically.

"What's going on in here?"

Jensen didn't answer. He just kept laughing as he pointed at Conrad's pants.

Conrad quickly turned to face her as he clenched the back of his pants, his face fire-engine red. "Uhhh... it looks like I had a little accident. I must've caught my pants on the corner of one of the drawers."

Sam felt bad for the poor guy but she couldn't keep from grinning. "I won't ask to see the damage but if you want to take them off in the bedroom, I might be able to sew them up."

He looked at her skeptically. "It'll only take a minute," she assured him.

The red-faced Conrad nodded in embarrassment and followed her to the bedroom.

Once inside, he closed the door and locked it. A few seconds later he opened the door a crack – just enough to toss the pants out and then quickly slammed it shut.

Sam quickly surveyed the damaged and hollered through the closed door, "I can fix these up in a jiffy. I'll be right back."

Conrad didn't answer. Instead, he swung the door wide open.

Sam's eyes got huge. She try to stifle a giggle but it was no use. She burst out laughing at the sight of Conrad.

Jensen and Andrea rushed into the hallway to find out what was so funny.

Instead of just waiting behind the door for his pants to get fixed, Conrad had found one of Sam's bathrobes and slipped it on. Well, maybe yanked would be a better word. It was a pretty pastel pink robe with little embroidered roses lining the collar and pockets.

Jensen slinked past Sam, his phone in hand. "Man, I gotta have a picture of this! The guys down at the station are going to love it!"

Andrea reached around and snatched the phone from Jensen's hand. "As much as I know you would *love* to do this to Conrad, I can't let you."

She turned to the nicely-robed officer and demanded, "Do you have any idea how ridiculous you look in that robe?"

She glanced over at Sam who was standing nearby and still giggling. "Not to say that it isn't a really *nice* robe..." She turned back to Conrad as she pointed, "It just doesn't look good on *you*!"

Jensen snickered. "You look like an overstuffed burrito, busting at the seams! Oh yeah, covered in Petunias!!" he added.

"Roses," Sam corrected.

"Go! Now! Take that ridiculous... uh, lovely robe off!!" Andrea looked over at Sam before continuing. "Before I change my mind and give Jensen his camera back!"

Conrad hung his head, turned around and shuffled back into the bedroom. The door quietly shut and they could hear him lock it – just in case.

Luckily, the tear in the pants was down the middle seam and a few minutes later Sam had them looking like new.

When Conrad came back out of the bedroom, he had his pants on and was looking sheepishly at Sam.

"I'm sorry for all the trouble, Mrs. Rite."

Sam waved a hand. "Please - call me Sam and it was no problem. Thank *you* for giving me a good laugh. It's been a trying day and I needed that!"

Jensen piped up. "Me, too." He looked at the ceiling, as if visualizing Conrad. "Man, that picture of you in that pretty pink bathrobe will be forever etched in my mind!"

Now that the pants crisis was over, Sam rustled up some sandwiches, chips and tea. They all sat on her back patio as they munched on their lunch. The three of them entertained Sam with stories of dumb criminals, kids' pranks gone wrong and other interesting stories of a cop's life. After listening to all that, she was glad that wasn't what she did for a living.

Half an hour later, they finished eating and made their way back inside. The living room was the last room to tackle – and it was the worst. Sam's heart sank. She'd been dreading this all day.

Michel managed to destroy all of her furniture except for a couple glass end tables. The front of the TV was ripped off, exposing the inside wires and the screen had a large crack that extended from one corner to the other. There was no chance of salvaging it.

Officer Barcheski shook her head in disgust. "I'm sorry to have to tell you it will probably take a couple weeks to process the damage report before you'll get reimbursed."

To Sam that wasn't important, even though it was going to be a big pain. She was just glad the most valuable items – the irreplaceable ones - were left unscathed.

Soon, the last room was in order, at least as much as it could be, and the three officers were gone.

Sam made a cup of hot tea and headed out to her back deck for a much-needed break. Just as she sat down, Lee called. "I got everything wrapped up here. I just talked to Lieutenant Barcheski. From what she told me, almost everything that was destroyed can be replaced." Lee sounded relieved.

"Mmm, hmm, yeah. I got lucky. They were a huge help today and I must admit - pretty entertaining."

Lee seemed distracted. "If you don't mind, I'm going to stop by. We were able to get quite a bit of information from Michel."

He arrived a short time later and as Sam opened the door to let him in, she could tell from the look on his face, something was wrong.

A shiver went down her spine. She wanted to get right to it so she quickly led him out onto the back patio.

As they sat down, Lee turned to Sam. "Before I go into too much detail, I have to ask a question. It's pretty important..."

He paused and Sam could tell he was searching for the right words.

He took a deep breath and continued. "This may sound like an odd question, but where's the luggage you brought back from the cruise?"

Something was very, very wrong. Sam searched Lee's face. Her eyes grew wide and her heart started pounding. The pieces were slowly starting to fall into place.

Michel had been searching for Sam's luggage! There was something in her luggage – maybe something he put there and now he wanted it back. He and more than likely others.

Sam stared at Lee intently. His expression was unreadable. She opened her mouth to speak but all that came out was a small squeak.

She shook her head as she tried again. "It's not here. Brianna borrowed it. She took it to Florida with her!"

Lee could hear the panic rising in her voice as she continued. "Tell me she's not in danger, Lee! Oh

Dear God in Heaven!" Sam mind was reeling and she felt like she was going to pass out.

Sheer terror began to set in. It was the same kind of feeling she had when Brianna was little and got lost in the mall. It was the panic she felt when the school called to tell her Brianna had been in an accident.

And it was a feeling of utter helplessness. Brianna was approximately 1200 miles away and Sam had given her something that had somehow put her in imminent danger.

Sam stood up, grabbed her cell phone and dialed Brianna's number. Busy signal. She tried again. Still a busy signal.

She suddenly remembered Jasmine and quickly dialed her number. Same thing!

Sam was shaking from head to toe. She had to know that her baby was OK!

Immediately, Lee was beside her. "Sam, sit down before you fall down. Please."

She obeyed instantly and dropped into her chair.

He gently squeezed her shoulder. "Stay here. I'll be back in five minutes."

He didn't have to worry about her going anywhere. She tried both girls' numbers again. Both lines were busy. She couldn't move, even if she wanted to. She was in shock, her mind completely empty.

As a last resort, she called the hotel. The operator put her call through to the girls' room but no one answered.

Sam barely noticed when Lee returned a short time later. He leaned forward and looked directly into her terror-filled eyes. "I have us on a direct flight to Orlando. It's leaving in two hours. Pack enough clothes to last a few days," he instructed her.

With that, he pulled her to her feet and started pushing her to the door as he continued talking, "Donovan is meeting us at the airport with my stuff. As soon as you're ready, we'll head over there."

The last part finally registered. She was on her way to Brianna! She didn't need to be told twice.

Within a few minutes, she managed to cram an overnight bag full of whatever her numb brain could think of. It didn't matter if she forgot something. She needed to get to her daughter – and fast!

In between packing, she kept trying to call Brianna and Jasmine but got the dreaded busy signal every time she tried.

They drove to the airport in silence. Lee kept glancing over at Sam. He could see she was still in shock. He reached over and grabbed her hand. "It will be OK. I know you can't focus right now but when we get on the plane and you can concentrate, I'll fill you in on the rest."

He tried to reassure her. "Don't worry. We'll find her safe and sound. I promise." The promise sounded hollow, even to him. He only wished he was as confident of that as he was trying to sound.

Sam turned to look over at Lee. Unshed tears filled her eyes and then slowly started to trickle down her cheeks. She opened her mouth to talk but only a gurgle came out so she closed it.

Lee couldn't see it but Sam had been praying the entire time. Really, she had been pleading with God, begging Him, bargaining with Him. Not her daughter. Not Brianna. If anything happened to Bri, Sam would never forgive herself. Her life would be over. There would be no reason to live.

The next hour was an absolute blur. Lee took control as Sam was in such a bad state-of-mind, she couldn't function. Her movements were almost robotic. By now, Lee began to worry that she wouldn't snap out of it.

What he didn't realize was that she was praying – and repeating the same scripture over and over in her head.

Psalm 91: 14-15. Because he hath set his love upon me, therefore I will deliver him: I will set him on high, because he hath known my name (15) He shall call upon me, and I will answer him: I will be with him in trouble: I will deliver him, and honour him. KJV

Brianna was in God's hands. She needed to grab hold of His promise of protection for her and her family.

As Sam meditated on the Word over and over, a look of peace and calm finally settled on her face.

Lee reached over and put his hand on her shoulder. "Whew! For awhile there, you had me worried."

Sam turned to Lee and simply said, "I've been praying and meditating on Psalm 91 and I'm finally feeling God's peace about the entire situation."

"Brianna will be just fine." To her it was a statement of fact.

Lee didn't answer. He believed in God. Well, he *had* believed in God – before He took his Annie away from him.

For a long time after her death he was mad. How could a loving God take away someone he loved so much? Annie never hurt anyone. She didn't deserve to die and she certainly didn't deserve to die the agonizing death she had.

Lee's pain was eventually replaced with an emptiness and he consciously shoved God into the dark, deep recesses of his mind.

As he looked at Sam, her empty expression was replaced by one of complete serenity. He hoped for all their sakes that she was right.

After they boarded the plane and settled into their seats, Lee took a deep breath and started to speak. "We believe Michel may have one or more accomplices..."

Chapter 10

Bri and Jasmine were up bright and early. They jumped out of bed and ran over to the window, pulling the thick, heavy curtains wide open. The palm trees were gently swaying in the breeze and the sun was shining brightly. Today was going to be a beautiful day!

The girls quickly got ready as they slipped into their swimsuits and beach covers and loaded up their beach bags before heading down to the lobby.

Travis and Luke were right on time and waiting for them. As they walked through the lobby, the girls quickly looked around. They never heard back from Jimmy and Vivian the night before and were relieved they were nowhere in sight this morning. There was just something about them that made them a bit uncomfortable ...

It was a short drive to Cocoa Beach. The girls pulled into the parking lot, right next to Luke's truck. They all got out and went around to the back. It was loaded with beach chairs, an umbrella, cooler, radio and blankets.

Bri and Jasmine looked at each other with blank stares. "Guess we weren't nearly as prepared…"

A sturdy beach cart hauled the gear through the hot sand until they all declared they had found the perfect spot to spread out. Half an hour later all the stuff was set up, sunscreen applied and the girls were dreamily gazing out at the deep, blue ocean.

Jasmine was the first to notice the huge waves crashing on shore. "Wow, are the waves always this big?"

Luke shook his head as he pointed to the red flags nearby. "No, we'll have to be careful today. Those huge waves can cause dangerous rip currents." He turned to the girls, his eyebrows raised, "Have you been watching the local news?"

When the girls admitted they hadn't, he explained there was a tropical depression brewing out in the Atlantic. The hurricane planes had been keeping a close eye on it and there was a good chance it would strengthen into a major storm. They still didn't know which direction it was going to take just yet, but there would be another update on the evening news.

Brianna's eyebrows furrowed as a look of worry crossed her face. "Jaz, we need to keep an eye on this!"

Travis agreed, "I would if I were you. They're saying it could be a big one."

By now, they were all starving so the guys unpacked the cooler they had brought with them. There were chicken tortilla wraps, wedges of watermelon and cantaloupe, small bags of chips, oatmeal raisin cookies and lots of Diet Coke and bottled water.

When they finished eating, and under the cautious eye of the nearby lifeguard, the girls tried their hand at catching some waves on the boogie boards. Everyone got a good laugh as they watched them try to balance on the small boards.

The sun was high in the sky by the time the afternoon thunderstorms rolled in off the water. The storms were moving fast so they quickly packed up the stuff and headed to their vehicles. It had been a perfect day and the girls were sorry to see it end.

Travis opened his truck door and paused just before jumping in. "Do you have any plans for tomorrow night?"

When the girls quickly shook their heads, he continued. "How about heading down to a few of the local clubs?'

The girls jumped at the offer! There was no need to even consult as they both nodded in unison.

It started to sprinkle and rumbles of thunder could be heard nearby. Luke turned a wary eye skyward before hurriedly adding, "Do you think it will be alright if we just pick you up at the hotel this time?"

Sure that the guys would now get the mom seal-of-approval, they both nodded again.

Kaboom! A bolt of lightning struck the water nearby. "OK, we'll see you at 6 then," Travis quickly added as he jumped in his truck and yanked the door shut.

Back on the main road, they were able to outrun the storm and pulled up in front of the hotel a short time later.

The girls struggled to carry all their beach gear and wet, sandy towels to the entrance. They made it safely inside just before the rain started pelting the pavement.

As the two of them dragged their stuff across the hotel lobby, they ran smack-dab into Jimmy and Vivian. The two were sitting on a sofa by the large front window, as if waiting for someone.

Bri and Jasmine looked at each other in disbelief. Could it really be that much of a coincidence they kept seeing them everywhere?

Jimmy jumped up as he spied Brianna first. "Hey you two. Sorry we missed you earlier. We were just sitting here wondering what we should do."

Vivian had joined him by then. "The desk clerk was telling us about a nearby Italian restaurant that has really good food – and it's cheap."

Jasmine set the heavy beach bag on the floor and shrugged her shoulders. There was no way out of it. They were cornered. "Uh, sounds good to me. What do you think Bri?"

Not knowing what to say, Bri replied, "Um, yeah. We hadn't really thought about dinner yet - but that sounds good."

After agreeing to meet downstairs in an hour, the girls hurried back to their room to shower and change. When they got inside, they noticed some of their stuff looked like it had been moved around.

Brianna walked to the door and pulled it open as she gazed at the sign still stuck in the top. "The do not disturb sign is still there. You don't suppose the cleaning lady came in here anyways..." her voice trailed off.

Just then, Jasmine noticed the balcony slider was open a crack. "Did you leave this open?"

Bri emphatically shook her head. "I'm sure it was locked when we left. I even double-checked."

Brianna shivered. "This is starting to creep me out. First we are being stalked by Jimmy and Vivian and now this."

The strange incidents were weighing heavy on them as they got ready for dinner and things seemed to get even more disturbing when they stepped out of the elevator and into the lobby.

The desk clerk spied the girls and quickly motioned for them to come over. When they got there, she began talking in a low voice. "I just thought I should let you know that someone called this morning. They asked if Brianna Rite was staying at this hotel." She paused before continuing. "I told them we aren't allowed to release guest information and they hung up on me."

Brianna's eyes grew wide as she looked over at Jasmine. They quickly thanked the clerk and walked away.

When they were out of earshot of the clerk, Jasmine spoke first. "Maybe we should call our parents and let them know weird things are happening."

Brianna shook her head. "But if we do that, they'll make us cut our trip short and come home," she reasoned. Neither girl was ready to leave, especially now that they had met Luke and Travis.

Just then an idea popped into her head. "My mom gave me the number for her friend Beth. She lives here in Orlando. Maybe we can call her later, tell her we're a little freaked out but don't want to tell my mom since she'll insist we come home. We can ask her to recommend a safe hotel in the area."

Jasmine looked relieved. "That's a great idea. We'll do it after we get back from dinner."

She frowned as a thought occurred to her. "But we've already paid for our room through tomorrow night. Why don't we just stay until then and move to another hotel after that?"

Before she could answer, Jimmy and Vivian stepped out of the elevator.

It was a short walk to the restaurant and the evening air was warm and inviting. They weren't the only ones enjoying the gorgeous weather. The sidewalks were full of people – mother's pushing strollers, couples holding hands, kids on skateboards, weaving in and out of foot traffic. It took a lot of people-maneuvering to avoid several near-collisions.

Vivian casually asked the girls what their plans were for the next day.

Oh no – not again!! Brianna quickly replied, "We're thinking about going to visit my mom's friend. She lives in the area."

Jimmy looked at her thoughtfully. "Really? And where does your mom's friend live?"

It struck her as odd that he pressed for details, so she was intentionally vague as she shrugged her shoulders and explained she didn't know yet. She didn't plan on giving him any more information and quickly changed the subject.

The restaurant was a great recommendation. The food was delicious and right in the girls' price range – cheap! The rest of the evening was uneventful and they had a good time. It made Brianna feel a little guilty of suspecting Jimmy and Vivian of being anything other than a nice, friendly couple trying to make friends.

The walk back to the hotel was uneventful and the girls said their good-nights to Jimmy and Vivian when they reached the hotel lobby.

Before heading up, they stopped by the front desk and asked the clerk if she had any more strange calls. She shook her head "no" which made the girls feel a little better.

When they finally got back to their room, the girls flipped on the TV for the first time since they arrived. The storm was all over the news. It had been upgraded to a Category 1 hurricane but it was too early to tell for sure which way it was headed. They were still in the potential path of the storm, but now they said there was a 50/50 chance it would completely miss them as it headed up the East Coast.

Even though that sounded like good news, the forecaster ended by saying that by tomorrow, the hurricane would gain strength and the winds would start to pick up, even if they didn't get a direct hit.

The screen flashed to a local home improvement store where people were lined up to buy flashlights, tarps and other stuff they might need if the storm was a direct hit. Jasmine turned up the volume.

The reporter was interviewing one of the men standing in the long line. Some of those reporter's questions were so dumb. "So are you worried that the hurricane will hit Central Florida?" *Duh, of course he was worried. Why else would he be in line buying emergency supplies?*

Jasmine shook her head. "What a stupid question!"

The reporter moved to an older, gray-haired lady that was behind him. "It looks like you're not going to wait to find out if we'll get a direct hit. What are you going to stock up on?"

Without hesitating the woman looked up at the reporter. "I'm hoping they have some generators left. I was here for the 2004 hurricanes and they were some of the worst storms I've ever seen. Never again will I wait until the last minute." She looked right into the camera before continuing. "Folks, this is nothing to mess with. You need to get ready now!"

The reporter seemed to like that answer as he turned back to the cameraman. "You heard it right here folks - from the voice of experience. Don't wait until it's too late."

Jasmine switched off the TV and plopped down on the edge of the bed. She glanced over at Brianna, a worried look on her face. "What if this thing ends up hitting us?"

Brianna tried to reassure her friend. "Even if it does, we'll be fine. They deal with these kinds of storms all the time down here. Try not to worry about it." Then she added, "Plus, we're not even sure it's coming this way."

Still, they were both a little more scared than they cared to admit. With that, they agreed to call Beth in the morning.   Maybe it would be a good idea to move on.

Neither one of them slept well that night as they tossed and turned. First it was the odd things happening to them and now they had to worry about a hurricane!

The first thing Brianna did when she woke up the next morning was pick up her phone and dial the number her mom had given her. When she didn't answer, Bri left a message.

Beth called back a short time later. Brianna confessed she and Jasmine were starting to stress out about the storm. For some reason, she stopped just short of mentioning the odd things that were happening.

Beth could hear the worry in Brianna's voice as she talked. "You girls can come stay with us. We have plenty of room." She paused before adding, "I insist!"

Bri looked uncertainly at Jasmine. "We've already paid for tonight – but maybe tomorrow if you don't mind?"

"That storm is far enough out that you'll be safe in the hotel tonight. So it's a deal. We'll see you tomorrow then – say around noon?"

She went on, as if she needed to convince Brianna it was a good idea. "If this storm does hit, there's a good chance the power will go out and you'll be trapped at the hotel since they'll only allow emergency vehicles on the road."

Brianna hadn't thought about that. Losing power and sitting in a hot, dark hotel room with a hurricane raging outside...

Brianna hung up the phone. It was time to call her mom. She was surprised when she didn't pick up so she left a voice mail and then sent her a text. Maybe she was with a client and couldn't talk, she reasoned.

It was Jasmine's turn to call home. Jasmine's mom picked up right away. She tried to sound casual as she mentioned the storm and the odd things that happened to them.

It didn't matter how nonchalant Jasmine tried to sound. Her mother was alarmed. "I think the best thing for you girls to do is come home. Orlando is a big city with so many different people. You might think you're safe but you can never be too careful."

She continued. "On top of that, I was just watching the weather myself. It's not just a "storm," Jasmine. This could turn into a major hurricane! If it does hit, they'll shut down the airports and you'll be trapped down there until it's over."

Jasmine interrupted her mom. "I know you want us to come back and I didn't mean to frighten you. We'll be fine. We're heading over to a friend of Samantha's first thing tomorrow morning." She added reassuringly, "We'll be safe there."

After a few more minutes of trying to convince Jasmine the best thing to do was come home, her mother gave up. It was no use. Her daughter was *so* stubborn sometimes!

Jasmine could hear the frustration in her voice. "If I can't talk you into coming home, please promise me you will be very careful. And call me when you get to the friend's house," she added.

She started to hang up. "Oh, mom!! If you talk to Brianna's mom, could you please tell her to call Bri? We haven't been able to get ahold of her and Bri is starting to worry."

Her mom agreed to pass the message along. With that, Jasmine was gone. She looked down at the phone in her hand and bowed her head to say a silent prayer for the girls' safety. A wave of anxiety rushed through her. Something didn't feel quite right and there was something the girls weren't telling her.

Jaz tossed the phone on the dresser and turned to Bri, "Sounds like this will be our last full day of fun. We better make the most of it."

They decided to skip the amusement parks and head to the outlet malls to go shopping instead. Money was getting low and they still needed to buy souvenirs for family.

When they got to the lobby level, they peeked around the corner before stepping out. No sign of

Jimmy and Vivian! With no time to lose, they made a swift beeline for the back door and moments later were safely inside their car.

The outlet mall was packed. You'd never know they were possibly in the path of a hurricane. It was a shopper's paradise! The girls were in heaven.

Store after store lined the outdoor mall. They seemed to have everything. Everything brand name, designer and best of all – at huge discounts! They both picked up expensive handbags for half price, got a great deal on some nice perfume and then each of them bought their moms a silk blouse.

By the time they made it all the way around the massive shopping center, they were groaning under the weight of all the treasures they'd found.

Brianna dropped her pile of bags for the umpteenth time as she tried to organize them. "Why, oh why, did I think I needed all this stuff?"

Jasmine was having difficulties of her own but somehow, the situation struck her as funny. She started giggling. "Just doing our part to help the local economy!"

She stretched her arms above her head as she looked around. "I think we're getting close to the car – at least I HOPE we're close!" This time they made note of where they parked before they started shopping.

They managed to gather up all their bags one last time and continue on. Thankfully, she was right and they were getting close to the car.

As they rounded the corner of the last building and faced the massive parking lot up ahead, they heard the "bonk-bonk-bonk" of someone's car alarm going off. But it wasn't just *anyone's* car alarm – it was theirs!

They picked up the pace, the car now only feet away. Brianna peeled the bags off her sore arms and quickly shoved her hand into her purse as she dug around for the keys.

The car alarm was driving her nuts! Finally, she found the right button and the annoying horn stopped.

She slowly approached the driver's side as Jasmine made her way to the passenger side. They cautiously bent down and peered inside. Still not sure the coast was clear, they pulled on the door handles. All four doors were still locked.

Jasmine glanced at Brianna over the roof of the car. "I didn't see anything. Did you?"

Brianna shook her head. "Me neither."

Back at the rear of the car, they scooped up all their bags and loaded them into the trunk. Jasmine stood there for a moment, admiring the cleanliness of it. "I wish my trunk was this clean."

Brianna nodded. "Yeah, me too. Mom's been on me to clean my car out."

After closing the trunk, they looked around before getting in. Once inside, they quickly locked the doors and turned on the car, cranking the air up to full blast.

Jasmine gave her friend a worried look. "This is really starting to freak me out."

Brianna decided a little pep talk was in order. "OK, let's not freak out. These are just odd little coincidences."

Jasmine wasn't convinced. "You're just trying to make me feel better!"

Brianna sighed. "I'm trying to make us *both* feel better."

Back at the hotel, they hauled their loot up to the room. Once inside, the girls looked around and let out an audible sigh of relief. Nothing looked out of place.

Brianna glanced down at the massive mound of bags piled high on the bed. "We need to figure out how we're going to get all this stuff into our suitcases!"

They spent the next hour pulling all their great finds out of the bags and showing them to each other. When Jasmine got to the new swimsuit she bought for herself, it gave her an idea.

"Hey, we haven't been to the pool yet. Let's go lay in the sun!"

It was the best idea they'd had all day and minutes later, they were lounging poolside, a tropical drink in hand.

"Cheers to your brilliant idea!" Brianna raised her glass to toast Jasmine.

Although the wind had picked up considerably, the sun was still shining brightly. It was hard to believe a hurricane might be on the way!

It suddenly dawned on Brianna that her mom had never called her back. The last she'd heard from her was a brief text the other morning.

She fished the phone out of her bag and dialed her mom's office number. When she didn't pick up, Bri left an urgent message to call her right away.

Next, she dialed the front desk of her mom's office. The receptionist informed her that her mother wasn't there. She hesitated for a second. "Your mom didn't come into work today. I'm not sure if she had a planned vacation day or called in sick but she hasn't been here."

Brianna frowned. Something was not right.

She thanked the receptionist and hung up. Panic filled her voice as she looked at Jasmine. "Mom didn't go to work today and she's not calling me back."

Jasmine could see her friend was really getting worried. "I'm sure she's OK. Someone would've called you by now if something was wrong..."

This made sense but still, she couldn't stop worrying.

The Florida sun was hotter than the girls were used to. After only a couple hours, they decided to head in.

Although Bri was still worried about her mom, she was also excited about seeing Travis again. He must have read her mind. Just then he texted, asking what time the girls would be ready and where they wanted to go.

Since the weather was a little iffy, they decided to stay close by and head over to BeachWalk to have dinner at one of the restaurants.

During dinner that evening, the girls shared with Luke and Travis all the odd things that were happening to them. Bri finished by telling them she couldn't reach her mom and was starting to get really worried.

Travis reached over and squeezed her hand. "I'm sure she's alright. Try not to worry."

"Maybe you two should move to a different hotel," Luke suggested.

Jasmine nodded. "We're checking out in the morning. We're going to stay with a family friend. Her name is Beth."

"Yeah, it's kind of funny. My Mom found out after she got back from her recent cruise that Beth and my Aunt Debbie had gone to school together," Brianna added.

Chapter 11

The plane had been in the air for over an hour. Lee reached over to grab Sam's hand. She was lost in her own world as she gazed mindlessly out the window. When she turned to Lee, the calm demeanor had disappeared. Her eyes were filled with tears, threatening to spill over at any moment. Lee put a finger under her chin. "Sam, you need to stop tormenting yourself. Brianna will be OK."

Sam shut her eyes tightly, the tears slowly making their way down her cheeks. When she opened them, Lee could tell she was listening to what he said. "Are you ready to hear the rest?"

She took a deep breath, wiped the trail of tears and slowly nodded her head.

"Good. This is important." He continued, "Michel carried the map onboard and his plan was to smuggle it into either Mexico or Belize."

"The original meeting was to take place in Mexico but at the last minute, Michel changed his mind."

"Sam, do you remember the masked man on the bus in Mexico that was looking for a Miguel? We're certain he was either looking for Michel or Miguel – the treasure map of the San Miguel."

He went on to say that a second rendezvous had been arranged in Belize where Michel was to exchange the map for the cash and for whatever reason, he changed his mind again.

"The only theory we could come up with is he must have discovered the map was worth huge amounts of money – money that he wanted to keep for himself."

Lee absentmindedly tapped his fingers on the tray in front of him. "So instead, he hid the map in your bag for safekeeping."

Sam interrupted Lee. "But I never saw anything in my bags that didn't belong to me."

"He used a special, secret compartment to conceal the map in the bottom of your suitcase. The compartment would be undetectable and easily blend into the lining of your bag. You wouldn't even notice unless you knew what you were looking for."

He stopped for a minute before going on. "The map is fairly large so we think he probably put it in the biggest bag you had."

Lee looked at Sam questioningly. "Was Michel ever in your room or did you ever give him access to your room where he might've had a chance to slip it in there?"

Sam's mouth dropped open as a light bulb came on. "I never let him in my cabin, but now that you say that, my room card came up missing one day when I was on deck reading a book." Her expression grew serious. "Right after Michel stopped by to say hello."

Lee nodded. "That's probably when he did it and you never even knew."

"When the abductors in Belize found out he didn't have the map, they threatened him. Told him he was to get the map and meet them in Miami within a week. Or they would hunt him down and kill him."

Lee looked at Sam. "That's why Michel was stalking you. He figured you still had the map and since you didn't know that it was hidden in your suitcase, he thought it would be easy to fly to Michigan, break into your house and get it back."

"What he didn't plan on was that the suitcase wouldn't be there. He tore your place apart looking for it and when he couldn't find it, he had to kidnap you to try and force you to tell him where the bag – and the map were at."

Sam looked confused. "But how did you find out he was stalking me?"

"From one of the abductors we interrogated in Belize. He never would tell us exactly why Michel was after you but we had a hunch. By the time I found out Michel was on his way to Michigan, there was no way I could make it there before him, so I sent Donovan in my place."

Sam leaned back in her seat as she tried to absorb everything Lee just told her.

As the plane got close to Florida, it started bouncing around, hitting several pockets of turbulence. Sam's palms were sweating as she whispered to Lee, "I hate flying!"

Lee grabbed Sam's hand and gave it a reassuring squeeze.

With less than an hour before their plane was scheduled to land in Orlando, the pilot made an announcement. "We've just received word that the Orlando airport has been closed due to poor weather conditions and our flight has been diverted to Jacksonville instead. I apologize for any inconvenience."

That was it. The end of the announcement. Everyone groaned.

Sam looked worriedly at Lee. "It'll be OK," he reassured her. "When we get there, we'll rent a car and head straight to Orlando. It's about a 3 – 4 hour drive, depending on traffic."

The pilot wasn't kidding. The weather in Jacksonville was getting iffy too, and the landing more than a little scary, which probably meant the *drive* to Orlando wasn't going to be much fun, either.

After they landed, Sam turned her phone back on and saw she had a message from Brianna. She listened to the call. She could tell from her daughter's voice that something was wrong. She immediately called her back but no one answered.

Sam listened to a second message. This one from Jasmine's mom. She mentioned the girls were a little spooked – something about odd things happening to them, like they were being followed - but not to worry – the girls were going to head over to a friend's house. Someone named Beth.

Chapter 12

KABOOM!!! Brianna sat upright in her bed. The wind was howling and something had just crashed into the building just outside their room.

She quickly grabbed the remote and flipped on the TV. There was an emergency broadcast on all channels. The storm had strengthened into a Category 3 hurricane and was on a direct path towards Cocoa Beach. From there, they projected it would head straight West and right into Orlando!

The weather man was highly animated as he exclaimed that outer storm bands were already, in fact, making their way inland as far as downtown Orlando. He seemed almost giddy.

She jumped out of the bed and raced over to where Jasmine was sleeping. She leaned over and started to shake her friend. "Jasmine, get up! The hurricane's coming this way! We need to get over to Beth's house right now!"

She grabbed her cell phone. No cell service whatsoever. She reached for the hotel phone. It was dead, too.

Jasmine was awake now. She grabbed her cell phone off the night stand and shook her head. Nothing.

The girls quickly dressed and threw everything into their bags. The hotel lobby was nearly deserted and it took only a couple minutes to check out.

The desk clerk shook his head as he handed them a receipt. "Are you sure you want to leave right now?"

There was no turning back. The girls nodded in unison as they headed toward the door.

They struggled to reach their car as the wind tried to push them back inside the building.

All around them they could hear branches snapping and loud banging, like doors slamming open and shut. Brianna glanced over to the edge of the parking lot. The strong winds were pushing a huge, metal trash bin into the side of a brick wall!

It took some doing, but the girls were finally safe inside the car. Wide-eyed, they looked at each other as if to say, "this can't be happening!"

Before pulling out of the parking lot, Jasmine punched Beth's address into the GPS and waited. It took forever but the directions finally popped onto the screen.

Bri let out a huge sigh of relief. It was only 30 minutes away!

The feeling didn't last long as she frowned and swallowed hard. "It looks like we'll be heading right into the eye of the storm!"

They cautiously pulled onto the main road. The streets were almost deserted. By the time they reached the highway, it was just about the same. They were pretty much the only ones on the road.

Jasmine started to panic. *What have we gotten ourselves into?* Maybe they should have just stayed at the hotel.

"Hopefully, Beth is home. I know she's expecting us." It still made Brianna a little nervous that she wasn't able to call and confirm. *What if she wasn't home??*

Soon, their exit was in sight and within a few minutes their car pulled onto Beth's street. They shook their heads and looked around in amazement. It was like a war zone! There were tree limbs lying all over, an empty trash can was rolling down the center of the road. Huge puddles of water covered large stretches of road. Not a single soul was in sight except them and another car that turned onto the street behind them.

Finally, they pulled up in front of what they hoped was the right house. The porch light was on – a good sign! "This is it. I hope they're home."

Brianna shut off the car and grabbed the door handle as she looked over at Jasmine. "Ready for this?"

Jasmine nodded. With that, the girls leaned on the doors, using all their strength to push them open just far enough to squeeze out.

The girls clung to the side of the car as they made their way to the rear. Brianna unlocked the trunk but the wind was too strong – they couldn't lift it open. It was as if someone had glued it shut!

Out of the corner of her eye, Jasmine saw something coming straight towards her. She quickly ducked. The object hit the ground nearby with a loud thud.

She looked at Bri, terror written all over her face. "That was a chunk of someone's metal shed. That thing could've cut my head off!"

It was obvious they wouldn't be able to get the trunk open so they linked arms as they began the treacherous journey to the front porch. The rain was coming down sideways as it pelted their faces and arms. It felt like a thousand needles were stabbing them.

After what seemed like hours, they finally reached the steps. The front door flew open. Brianna recognized Beth from the pictures her mom had shown her. She was so relieved she almost had a melt-down right there on the porch.

Beth's tall, slender frame filled the doorway. She reached out to grab Brianna's hand. "Quick, get in here before something takes one of you out." The girls were pulled inside and the door quickly slammed shut.

Jasmine shuddered. "Yeah, like a giant piece of flying metal!"

Beth looked them up and down. The girls were soaked to the skin, huge puddles of water forming on the floor around them. "You two look like you just went through an automatic car wash – minus the car!"

Jasmine grimaced. "Yeah, that's about what it felt like."

Beth turned to Brianna, "I was going to call your mom but our phones are out. Were you able to get through?"

Bri shook her head. "No, neither of us have service. I haven't talked to her in a couple days." Her lower lip started quivering as tears welled up in her eyes.

Beth could see she was visibly shaken and upset. "Don't worry, I'm sure she knows you're fine. You look like a smart girl, one that has enough sense to stay safe."

Before Brianna could answer, Beth turned and yelled to someone they couldn't see. "Tom, go grab the girls' bags before it gets any worse out there."

Jasmine shook her head, "Oh, you don't have to do that. We don't need them right now."

Beth was determined. "Nonsense, it will only take him a minute. They'll be safer in here than they will be in the car."

Tom soon appeared from out of the hallway, dressed in a long trench coat and rubber boots. He was not smiling as he nodded at the girls.

Jasmine felt bad. "Really, it's not necessary. There's nothing in the suitcases that we need to have."

Beth wouldn't hear it. "Don't you worry about him. He'll be back in no time. Just a little wind and rain."

The girls look at each other in disbelief. *Just a little wind and rain??*

Tom stepped around the girls. He took a deep breath and yanked the front door open. As soon as his feet hit the porch, they started to close the door behind him. It took all three of them to push it shut.

He was back a short time later, struggling as he tried to cram all their bags through the small opening at the same time.

By now, the girls were sitting on the couch. When they saw how much grief their bags were causing, they rushed over to try and help.

Beth got there at the same time. She quickly snatched one of the bags out of Brianna's hands. "No need to mess with these right now. I'll just take them to the bedroom for you. Be right back."

Jasmine glanced at Bri with a look that said she's either super-hospitable or a bit overbearing. Tom didn't follow his wife. Instead, he stood there staring at the girls, not saying a word.

Brianna started to feel uneasy, like Tom resented their presence.

Suddenly, Beth hollered out from the back of the house. "Tom, can you come back here for a minute?"

He glanced over at the girls one last time before he disappeared in the direction of Beth's voice.

After he was gone, Jasmine whispered. "That was odd."

Brianna nodded. "There's something weird about the whole get-our-luggage-and-run-to-the-bedroom-thing."

Before Jasmine could reply, both Beth and Tom returned to the room. Instead of sitting down she headed in the direction of what had to be the kitchen. "Well, I'm sure you girls must be starving. Come on! I'll fix you a sandwich."

She didn't wait for an answer and continued walking. It didn't leave them much choice but to follow.

The girls hopped onto the barstools as Beth started making small talk, asking what the girls had done while they were in town and if they'd made any friends.

Jasmine breathed a sigh of relief. Finally, a normal conversation! They told her about the beach, meeting Luke and Travis. Brianna started to mention Jimmy and Vivian but something told her to keep quiet, so she changed the subject.

Beth paused mid-sandwich, the mayo-covered knife still in her hand as she turned her gaze to Brianna. "You were going to say something?"

Brianna looked down, her mind racing. "Oh, I lost my train of thought. This storm has me rattled!"

That answer seemed to satisfy Beth and she turned back to making the sandwiches. Brianna glanced at Jasmine, their eyes met and Jasmine faintly shook her head. Something still didn't feel right with these two.

After they finished eating, Beth led them back into the living room. Jasmine was just about to sit down when she had a thought. "I'd like to grab my cell phone out of my bag – just in case it starts working again. Which room are the bags in?"

Beth led her to the hallway and stopped. She motioned to one of the rooms. "They're in the last room on the right. I set them on the bed."

The words were no more out of her mouth and Jasmine was halfway down the hallway, hoping that Beth wouldn't decide to follow her.

When she reached the bedroom, she switched on the light and started walking towards the bags. She gazed around the room. There was a telephone sitting on the nightstand. Hmmm... She glanced behind her to see if anyone was around. Certain she was alone, she walked over to the phone, gently lifted the receiver and put it to her ear. Her eyes widened. There was a dial tone!

Jasmine's heart started pounding and she started to feel sick. *Remain calm*, she told herself. *Maybe it **wasn't** working when Beth tried it earlier*, she reasoned.

There was only one way to find out. She quietly put the receiver back in its place, grabbed her cell phone and returned to where the others were waiting. She pretended to check for cell service. "Still no service. I wonder if your phones are still down..." her voice trailed off.

Beth was standing at the front window looking out. She turned to Jasmine as she shook her head. "No, they're still not working. I checked just a minute ago."

She's lying! I knew it. Jasmine's mind was racing. *Why doesn't she want us using her phone?*

Just then the lights flickered and then went out. Tom, being ever-so-observant, stated the obvious. "Power's out." He walked into the kitchen and quickly returned with several flashlights. "Looks like we'll need these."

Brianna thanked him as she turned it on and stood up. "Can I use your restroom?"

Jasmine saw her opportunity and quickly stood up, too. "Yeah, I need to go, too."

Beth pointed in the direction of the hallway. "It's down there on the left hand side."

Both girls headed in that direction with Jasmine right on Bri's heels.

Brianna was annoyed. "What are you doing??" she whispered angrily.

Instead of answering, Jasmine practically shoved her into the bathroom and quickly closed the door.

Brianna couldn't believe Jasmine was acting so weird. "What are you doing?" she repeated.

Jasmine's face was only inches from Brianna's when she whispered. "Their phones work! When I came back to get my cell phone, I saw a house phone sitting on the nightstand so I picked it up, and there was a dial tone!"

Brianna was skeptical. "Are you *sure*?"

"Yes, of course I'm sure!"

"What are we going to do?"

"What can we do? We're in the middle of a hurricane!"

Brianna being the ever-practical one. "Let's just wait here until the storm ends and then make an excuse to leave as soon as possible." It sounded like a good idea to her.

Jasmine paused. You couldn't argue with common sense. "I guess that'll have to be good enough." Plus, they really didn't have a choice.

The girls turned to go. Just then there was a sharp cracking noise right outside the window that was way too close for comfort. They yanked the bathroom door open and scurried back to the living room.

When they got there, Tom and Beth were bent over, talking in low voices. They immediately stopped when they saw the girls. Several candles were now flickering on the coffee table.

The girls sat down uncomfortably on the loveseat, unsure of what to say next. They all sat there in silence for several minutes as they listened to the wind whipping outside. There was an almost non-stop banging noise, like something was hitting the side of the house.

Brianna silently prayed that the storm would end soon. She couldn't wait to get out of there.

Chapter 13

The closer Sam and Lee got closer to Orlando, the worse the storm became. They were driving right into the eye of a hurricane. Lee looked over at Sam. "Can you grab my phone and see if I have service?"

Sam shrugged skeptically. "I doubt it. I keep checking mine and nothing."

She fished it out of the console and glanced down. Shocked, she saw that he had three bars! "You have service! Quick, call someone!"

"I don't want to take my eyes off the road. Can you scroll down and find the number for Poker Face? He's my inside guy down here. Hopefully he'll have some good news."

Sam glanced sideways at Lee. *Odd name. Poker Face.* She pressed the call key and handed the phone to Lee.

Whoever it was picked up right away. "Hey, I have cell service but not sure for how long. What do you have?"

Lee listened intently for several minutes. Every once in a while he would comment or agree with whatever "Poker Face" was saying. He pulled the phone away from his face and looked over at Sam. "Take this down."

He returned to his conversation. "OK. Give me the address. We're still about an hour away. Hopefully the roads are clear and we can get through." With that, he rattled off an address that Sam quickly wrote down.

"No, don't wait for us. If you have a chance..." His voice trailed off. He pulled the phone from his ear. He looked disappointed. "Lost service."

Sam had a thousand questions. "Where are we going? Did you find out anything? Are the girls safe?"

Lee turned to Sam. "As far as we know. My inside guy has a stakeout on them **and** the bad guys that are looking for the map. Unfortunately, they're all together," he finished.

Sam's mind was reeling. "Have the girls been abducted?"

Lee shrugged then shook his head and answered honestly. "I'm not sure."

The storm was finally easing up. At least there was no more pounding noises on the side of the house. It was getting really dark inside Beth's house and the candles were giving off an odd glow that bounced off Beth and Tom's faces.

Jasmine shuddered. It reminded her of zombie creatures. She made a silent pact with herself to stop watching scary movies.

Brianna suddenly stood up. "I've got something in my eye. I'm going to grab some contact lens stuff." Jasmine stood up, too. "I'll go with you."

Without giving Tom and Beth a chance to reply, they swiftly walked towards the hallway. They could feel two sets of eyes boring into their backs as they left the room.

When they got to the back bedroom, Brianna turned to Jasmine. "We need to get out of here."

"How are we going to do that?" Jasmine looked around. "Hey, all our stuff is back here. Why don't we just sneak out the bedroom window and make a run for the car?"

Brianna laughed. "That's a little dramatic. Maybe we should just grab our stuff, walk to the front door, and tell them that now the storm is letting up we're leaving?"

She stuck her hand on her hip. "It's not like they're going to *kidnap* us!"

They started bickering as neither one liked the other's idea.

Just then, there was a loud commotion coming from the front of the house. It almost sounded like the front door had been kicked in.

Seconds later, they heard glass breaking. It sounded like it was coming from the direction of the kitchen.

Jasmine whispered loudly. "Holy Smokes! Something's going on out there."

She grabbed Bri's arm. "See? I told you we should've gotten out of here when we had a chance!"

There was no time to discuss it now! The girls looked at each and had the same exact thought. Dive under the bed! They hit the ground and rolled under.

In the meantime, they could hear yelling and cursing coming from the living room. A woman let out a bloodcurdling scream.

The girls reached for each other's hand as they squeezed their eyes tightly shut and sucked in a breath.

As suddenly as the noise started, it stopped. They lay very still, not moving an inch. After what seemed like forever, they heard footsteps coming down the hall.

Someone was calling their names. "Brianna, Jasmine, are you in here?"

Brianna put a finger to her lips. Jasmine clamped her mouth shut and held her breath. A beam of light was bouncing around the room. Someone was looking for them! It didn't take long for the light to slowly lower to the floor as it came to rest on them, shining right in their eyes.

"You can come out now." The light was blinding. They couldn't see who was talking but the voice sounded vaguely familiar. Their hiding place discovered, there was nothing left to do but crawl out from under the bed.

The girls stood up and brushed off their clothes. Acting braver than she felt, Jasmine turned her flashlight on and shined the light towards the door. Her hand flew to her mouth as she let out a gasp. A look of shock plainly etched on her face. It was Jimmy!

He was smiling at them. "I'm sure you're surprised to see me!"

Surprised didn't come close to describing it. Speechless – yes, that was the word. Without waiting for them to answer, he headed for the door and motioned for them to follow.

The girls looked at each other. They really didn't have much of a choice. He led them back into the living room. It was a mess. Tables were knocked over, shattered glass covered the dining room floor. The front door was hanging on its hinges as rain poured in.

Brianna looked around in disbelief until her eyes settled on Beth and Tom. They were handcuffed and sitting silently on the couch.

Besides Jimmy, there were three other people standing in the living room. And one of them was Vivian. When she saw the girls staring at her, she walked over and put a hand on Brianna's arm. "You guys OK?"

They nodded in unison. "Yes, we're fine." They weren't sure what else they could say. None of this made sense.

Why were Beth and Tom handcuffed on their couch and what did that have to do with Jimmy and Vivian? And how did Jimmy and Vivian end up *here?*

Vivian looked from one to the other. It was obvious from the look on the girls' faces, they had no idea what was going on.

She turned to Brianna. Maybe this would help. "Your mom is on the way. She and Lee will be here any minute."

Brianna stared blankly, her words not registering. *Her mom was here? In Florida?* Vivian repeated her words, hoping this time they would sink in. "Brianna, you mom is only minutes away."

Finally, she got it. Brianna had never been so happy in her life! Both girls started to cry as they hugged each other.

Vivian reached over and patted Jasmine on the back. "I know this is all confusing to you but really, it's going to be OK."

It wasn't twenty minutes later that a car pulled up out front. Brianna's mom jumped out as the vehicle rolled to a stop. She darted up the front steps, a tall man right on her heels.

When Sam reached the door, her eyes frantically scanned the room. They finally settled on Brianna and she raced over to wrap her arms around her daughter's trembling shoulders.

Brianna hugged her mom tightly. It felt wonderful. She hoped her mom would never let go.

But she did. Next she grabbed Jasmine and gave her the same smothering mom hug. Jasmine drew a shaky breath, tears filling her eyes. "I am so glad to see you, Mrs. Rite!"

"Not as glad as I am to see you two!" Brianna's mother replied. After a few more hugs, Sam finally let the girls sit down.

She turned to the tall man who had come in behind her and was now standing quietly nearby.

"Brianna, you finally get to meet Lee." Sam pointed at the girls. "Lee, this is my daughter, Brianna, and her best friend, Jasmine."

Besides being very tall, one of the first things Brianna noticed were his incredible green eyes. She tried not to make it too obvious as she closely studied him. Tall, yes. Handsome and very muscular, too. Well, her mother certainly had good taste!

Finally, she smiled at him, giving her seal of approval. He smiled back and let out the breath he had been unconsciously holding.

She held out her hand. "Nice to meet you." Looks like he had passed inspection!

Jasmine stood up and wiggled her way between them. "My, my Mrs. Rite. You certainly have good taste!"

"Jasmine, you are such a flirt!" Brianna shook her head at her friend but she was smiling.

Lee laughed. Sam blushed. "Thanks Jasmine, and yes, I think I do, too."

The introductions over, they all turned to look at Tom and Beth sitting silently on the couch. Now the center of attention, Beth glared at Sam and Lee. "You ruined everything. You and your disgusting daughter."

That was the last straw. Sam was furious! She marched over and planted herself directly in front of Beth. She crossed her arms and bent down so that she was eye-level. "It's a good thing these girls weren't harmed. If you had so much as touched a hair on either one of their heads, I would have hunted you down to the ends of this earth!"

Whoa! Brianna's eyes grew wide as she stared at her mother. Her mom was always so sweet and nice to everyone. This was a side she'd never seen!

Jimmy and Vivian had been standing off to the side quietly observing. Finally, it was time to make their presence known. Lee looked over at them and nodded.

Sam suddenly felt someone standing directly behind her. She spun around to see who it was.

Jimmy?? Vivian?? Her jaw dropped. Her legs started wobbling so she reached out and grabbed the edge of the couch. Her hand flew to her mouth, her eyes shocked wide-open.

"You're alive." Samantha grabbed Vivian's arm. "I can't believe it. You're alive!"

She turned to Jimmy. "I don't understand..."

She wasn't the only one. Brianna was more confused than her mother. "Mom, you *know* them?"

Lee walked over to mother and daughter. "I'm sure you're both confused and I can explain everything..."

Just then, a marked police car pulled up and two uniformed officers stepped in to take Beth and Tom away.

But not before Lee stopped them as they were being led out the front door. "You might as well tell us where the map is. If not," he waved his hand in the direction of Sam and the girls, "we will take great pleasure in tearing every inch of your house apart – just like Michel did to Sam's."

Beth clamped her mouth shut but Tom just shrugged. "There's a framed picture of a palm tree over our master bed. We hid the map and list in the back."

Without saying a word, Lee nodded his head at the police and Tom and Beth were gone.

Brianna turned to Sam questioningly. Her mom sighed. "It's a long story. I'll try to explain it on the way to the hotel."

But first, Sam had questions of her own. Lee had no sooner started the car when Sam began firing away.

"So Jimmy and Vivian were part of the rescue team in Belize?"

Lee nodded. "Yeah, I couldn't blow their cover. They're actually detectives. When the captors realized the two of them weren't just innocent tourists, they dragged them from the tent that night."

He continued. "When that happened, it was time to make our move. Their lives were in danger."

Sam shook her head in wonderment. "So they were keeping an eye on the girls down here, too?"

"In a roundabout way. Their real reason for being here was to keep an eye on Beth and Tom. We suspected they had something to do with the map and Michel."

Sam interrupted, "But what about Emily, Beth's daughter?"

"Completely innocent. She had no idea what was going on."

Sam crossed her arms, a thoughtful look on her face. "Hmm... I feel like I'm in a movie."

It was the middle of the night by the time they made their way to the hotel and checked in.

Sam turned to Lee, "I better keep an eye on these two – make sure they stay out of trouble."

Brianna rolled her eyes at her mom's words. "Sounds like you're the one that got me in trouble in the first place."

She quickly changed the subject. "Hey, now that you're here, you can meet Travis. Jasmine and I both met someone."

Ahhh, to be young again! Now it was her mother's turn to roll her eyes.

"No Mom. You're really going to like them." She was rattling on. Sam glanced at Lee over the top of Bri's head. "See you in the morning," she mouthed.

Once inside their room, it didn't take long to unpack. Sam packed in such a hurry, she had only a handful of clothes.

Jasmine and Brianna were so excited and relieved, they chattered on and on about their trip, the boys they met, their plans for tomorrow. Finally, they settled down and drifted off to sleep.

Sam checked her phone one last time before turning in. She smiled as she looked at a text Lee sent. "Sorry I didn't get to give you a proper good-night kiss... I'd like to take a rain check, if you don't mind... "

She had a second text that read: "I have a meeting in the morning to go over what happened today and I'll have to turn in the map. If you and the girls would like to take a peek at it before I leave tomorrow, I'll meet you in the dining room downstairs for breakfast around 9."

She quickly replied. "Yes, we would love to see what caused us all so much grief! It's a date! We'll see you at 9."

She hit send. There was one final text, leaving no room for doubt. "And I'll be holding you to your promise for that kiss!" She hit send one more time, plugged the phone into the charger and shut off the light.

A smile etched on her face as she snuggled under the covers and nodded off.

Sam woke to a bright ray of sunlight shining right in her eyes. Apparently the girls hadn't done a very good job of shutting the drapes the night before and light was pouring in the room.

Sam squinted at the clock beside her bed. 7:30 a.m. *Might as well get up. Three girls and one bathroom. We'll need that hour and a half just to get ready.*

She looked over at the two lumps in the other bed, their bodies completely covered. Sam shook her head. *That would give me a major claustrophobic panic attack!*

She quietly grabbed her bag and tip-toed to the bathroom. Thirty minutes later she was showered and dressed, her hair pulled back in the customary ponytail.

She looked at the girls again and shook her head. Still sound asleep. "Time to rise and shine sleeping beauties. We have a busy day today. You both have one hour to get ready so we can meet Lee for breakfast!"

Bri peeked out from under the covers as she opened one eye and groaned. Jasmine rolled over and burrowed even deeper under the covers. For good measure, she threw her pillow on top.

Sam stuck her hands on her hips. *This ought to get them motivated.* "Well, you don't have to get up, but Lee said this would be our only chance to see the treasure map before he has to turn it in later this morning."

That was all she needed to say. The girls both jumped up at the same time. Who *wouldn't* want to see a treasure map that was worth millions of dollars?

An hour later, they were seated in the dining room, waiting for Lee to arrive. The smells were torturing them as they suddenly realized they were starving. Over the last few days, stress had taken their toll and food had been one of the last things on any of their minds.

Sam glanced around. "Looks like they have a pretty good variety on the breakfast buffet. Maybe we should just get that ..."

Just then, Lee walked in. He gave both girls a quick hug hello and then leaned over to plant a gentle kiss on Sam's cheek. "Good morning beautiful ladies." Sam turned a slight shade of pink.

Brianna snorted as she looked over at her mother. "Ha! You made my mom blush!"

"I haven't seen your mom look this happy in a long time!" Jasmine chimed in.

Sam put her hand up. "OK, now stop embarrassing me – all of you!"

"We're having the breakfast buffet," Jasmine informed Lee.

He nodded as he glanced in that direction. "Sounds good."

After the waitress took their order, Brianna couldn't stand it any longer. "Where is it?" she demanded.

"Ah, a woman of few words. I like that," Lee joked. He reached down and pulled a manila file folder from the bag at his feet. By now he had all three girls' undivided attention. They couldn't *wait* to see what the map looked like.

Lee carefully unfolded the crinkled brown paper and spread it out in the middle of the table. It wasn't too big – roughly the size of a large picture - but it looked ancient. The edges were jagged and blackened like someone might have tried to burn it at one time.

They all leaned in to get a closer look. In the right hand corner was a compass. In the left hand corner was a small scale, marking distance.

In the center of the map was a rough sketch –
an outline of the State of Florida. Several palm trees
dotted the landscape. The words "Florida" and "St.
Augustine" were written on the map by a shaky hand.
The letters were not straight and the words almost
unintelligible, badly faded over time. Crude waves,
indicating the Atlantic Ocean were sketched to the
right of what was marked as St. Augustine.

Just above St. Augustine, a dotted line had
been drawn, curving upward into the ocean. There
were three lines in all – extending roughly two inches
out into the water. At the end of the dotted line was a
wooden ship with an "X" beside it and in very small
letters were the words "hundido aquí." Lee
translated. "That's Spanish for - sunk here."

"Whatcha lookin' at?" All four of them
jumped! The waitress was peeking over Sam's
shoulder. They were so focused on the map, they
hadn't heard her return.

Lee quickly pulled the map from the table and
shoved it onto his lap. "Oh, just a little souvenir we
picked up."

Sam quickly hid her smile as the girls looked at Lee with an admiring glance. *Wow, good one.*

After the waitress finally walked away, Lee turned to the girls again. "Would you like to see the ship's manifest?

All three nodded in unison. Lee carefully placed the map back in the folder and pulled out another paper. He once again set it in the center of the table, careful to keep it away from the brimming coffee cups.

The list was on the same old, brown paper. It was obvious from the handwriting, it was written by the same person – in very sloppy, crooked letters. The list included Tobacco, Spices, Indigo, Silver, Gold, Diamonds, Pearls, Emeralds and other valuable gems.

"Fascinating," Sam murmured.

Lee finally put the list back in the folder and carefully slid it into the bag.

The girls looked at Lee curiously. Brianna leaned forward, talking in a hushed voice. "So this treasure is still out there? If a survivor of the San

Miguel drew that map after the ship sunk, there's a pretty good chance that ship is close to where he marked it?"

Lee nodded. "That's what I think."

Jasmine spoke up. "We should go look for it. Think of how rich we would be!" Her eyes stared dreamily off into the distance.

Food overruled riches and with that, the girls remembered they were starving to death. They grabbed their plates and headed to the buffet.

As they walked away, Lee turned to Sam. "I think they're onto something. Wouldn't mind looking for it myself," he added thoughtfully.

Before Sam could answer, they were back, their plates piled high. There were omelets, toast, bacon, sausage, hash browns, cheese-filled Danish.

Sam eyed the food. "That looks so good! Now it's our turn." They both pushed back their chairs and stood.

Not trusting the precious documents out of his sight, Lee grabbed the bag and slung it over his shoulder. He looked at the girls. "I trust you but I certainly don't trust anyone else," nodding towards their waitress.

Bri shook her head. "I wouldn't either, considering all we've gone through for that crazy thing."

They enjoyed a leisurely breakfast before Lee finally stood up as he looked at his watch. "Better get going or I'll be late. The sooner I get this thing off my hands, the better."

He glanced at Sam. "I'll see you later tonight?"

Sam smiled warmly. "Yes, of course."

She turned to the girls. "We can't wait to meet your new friends. Would it be possible for all of us to have dinner tonight?"

"We'll have to double-check, but that shouldn't be a problem," Jasmine replied.

On the way back to the room, Sam asked the girls what their plans were for the day. Brianna spoke first. "Well, with the storm damage, we're not sure what kind of shape the parks are in."

"Honestly," she confessed, "we've had enough excitement to last us awhile. We would be just as happy hanging out here at the hotel."

Jasmine chimed in. "Since you upgraded us to such a nice hotel, I think we'll just stay around here today."

Sam nodded. "I agree. Then I won't have to worry about what you're doing and what kind of trouble you might be getting into..."

Bri frowned at her mother. "Well, if not for you and your stinkin' treasure map."

Sam laughed at her daughter's annoyed expression. "I know, I know. I'm teasing."

Bri quickly smiled and hugged her mom. "I'm glad you're here."

"Me too, Mrs. Rite," Jasmine chimed in as she hugged Samantha.

"Speaking of that, have you called your mom, Jasmine?"

Jasmine promptly called her mom.

The girls spent the rest of the day lazing by the pool, enjoying the warm sunshine and working on their tans. It was hard to believe a hurricane had just gone through!

Later that afternoon, Sam ran upstairs to grab more sunscreen. She suddenly remembered her cell phone that was charging on the nightstand. She picked it up and saw a number she didn't recognize.

Curious, Sam listened to the message. *Well, I'll be darned.* She rolled her eyes.

"Yeah, hey Sam. Gabby here. I know this is probably a surprise – me calling you out of the blue and all. I hope you don't mind…"

"I know your daughter is here – or was here – kinda scoping out the place, you know, cuz y'all are thinking of moving down and – I think that would be GREAT! I mean, I've only been here a few weeks myself and I haven't really met too many people."

"Anyways, I'm sorry to be ramblin' on. Just kinda lonely, ya' know. So, uh, if you have time… you know… whenever, give me a call. OK? Thanks. Bye!"

Sam started to feel guilty. *Poor Gabby. Nothing like being in a new place and not having any friends. I ought to give her a call. Maybe I can have lunch with her before I head back home.*

Before she could change her mind, she dialed Gabby's number and wasn't surprised when she picked up after only one ring.

"Hi Sam! Wow, thanks for calling me back! How ya doin'? Is your daughter still in town?" Gabby didn't give Sam a chance to get in a word edgewise.

She sounded so excited to hear from Sam, it made her feel even worse for rolling her eyes and feeling exasperated.

When Gabby finally stopped to catch her breath, Sam quickly spoke up. "Believe it or not, I'm actually in Orlando for a couple days myself. Maybe we can have lunch..."

Before Sam could even finish her last sentence, Gabby was back. "Yeah! Yeah! I would LOVE that!" she gushed.

They talked for a few more minutes. It was obvious that Gabby was really lonely. Before hanging up, they made tentative plans for dinner the following evening with Sam promising to call her back as soon as she talked to Lee.

On her way back down to the pool, Sam had a crazy idea. Not just *any* crazy old idea but a really great, maybe-I-should-be-a-matchmaker-idea. She couldn't wait to talk to Lee!

She settled back down in her lounge chair, pleased-as-punch with herself.

Brianna hopped out of the pool and ran over to Sam. "Travis and Luke can meet us for dinner. I told them 7 tonight at the International Grille – just down the road." Pleading eyes stared down at Sam.

"Yes, of course. That sounds perfect!"

Lee texted her shortly after with a two-word message. "Mission Accomplished." Sam let out an audible sigh of relief. She was so glad the map was gone and she didn't have to worry about it anymore. Maybe their lives could get back to normal now – whatever that was!

She relayed the message on the dinner plans for 7. She no more than hit send when her phone rang. It was Lee letting her know he was wrapping things up and should be back to the hotel earlier than he thought - somewhere around 5.

Hmm, he would be back early! Sam had an idea. "Since we're not meeting the kids for dinner until 7:00, why don't we meet out by the pool bar around 6 for a little alone-time?"

Lee laughed. "Great minds think alike. I was just going to suggest the exact same thing."

Sam smiled slyly to herself as she hung up. This would give her a chance to casually mention dinner tomorrow night with Gabby!

Later that afternoon, Sam left the girls fussing over themselves in the bathroom. She rehearsed in her head how she was going to pitch the dinner-thing as she headed down to the meeting place.

Lee was already waiting for her. Sam's eyes lit up when she spotted him. *Such a good looking guy – what is he doing with me?*

Lee stood when he saw her coming. He took Sam's hand as he pulled her forward and gave her a tender kiss. "Hey beautiful lady. I missed you today."

Sam blushed and glanced down at her outfit. The girls had talked her into wearing one of Bri's cute little summer skirts and sleeveless blouses. The colors were bright and tropical – not something Sam would normally pick out for herself.

She wrinkled her nose and twirled around. "These are Brianna's clothes. You don't think they look too young ..." she trailed off.

Lee grabbed her waist and pulled her close. His eyes crinkled into a smile. "I think you look breathtaking!"

He bent down and kissed her hard, his arms closing around her. For a minute, Sam completely forgot they were in a very public place.

"Ahem. Can I get you two lovebirds something to drink?" Lee reluctantly pulled away and glanced over Sam's head at the bartender. "I think my beautiful girlfriend will have a glass of Chardonnay. I'll take a light beer."

He just called her his *girlfriend!* Sam's heart skipped a beat, a bright smile lighting her face.

"So you don't think the outfit is too much?" She didn't give him a chance to answer before she continued. "I was just thinking how handsome you look. Every time I see you, you look different somehow."

Tonight he had on a pair of khaki dress shorts and a short sleeve polo shirt that were the exact same color as his mesmerizing green eyes. He finished the look with a pair of casual Teva sandals.

Just then, the bartender returned with their drinks. Lee lifted his beer in a toast. "Here's to the end of another great adventure!"

Sam lightly tapped his mug with her wine glass and cleared her throat. "Great adventure for you, maybe. Another nail biter for me. I think I'll take a break from danger and excitement for a while!"

Lee leaned back in his chair and laughed. "Well, if you hang around me long enough, it will happen again! Probably sooner than later," he admitted.

He leaned in closer and looked around to see if anyone was listening. "I turned in the map but before I did, I took a few pictures of it." He patted the phone in his pants pocket.

"Don't you think it would be exciting to search for the treasure? I've always wanted to do that."

Sam could see the wheels spinning in his head. "I did some digging. Whatever we find would be ours to keep. As a Navy Seal, I have extensive dive experience. This would be a great adventure!"

Lee sobered. "Sam, knowing the location of the sunken ship, we could be millionaires. We would never have to worry about money!"

Sam gazed thoughtfully at Lee. "But don't you think the government will be hot on it if they think the map is legit?"

Lee shook his head, laughing. "Have you ever seen the government do anything in a big hurry?"

Sam had to admit he was probably right. "Yeah, you're right." Her brows furrowed. "You won't be in any danger?"

He looked at her with a serious expression on his face. "Everything is dangerous. Walking out of here and crossing the street could be dangerous."

He paused. His voice grew excited. "I just think this would be the opportunity of a lifetime."

He went on to explain that his great-grandfather had been a gold miner in Alaska and when he was young, he heard the stories of how much money could be made digging for gold.

Sam didn't have the heart to burst his bubble so she stayed quiet. Worried but quiet.

He went on, "I already talked to Donovan. He's up for an adventure and agreed to go with me."

Donovan! With all the talk of treasure, she almost forgot and now was the perfect time to ask!

Sam tried to sound casual as she glanced down at her drink. "So, is Donovan in town now?"

Lee nodded. "Yeah. He's back. We're going to get together and start planning the dive."

Sam looked up at Lee expectantly. "I was just thinking ... it would be nice to have dinner with him ... you know ... thank him for all his help and see him one last time before I have to fly back to Michigan. Maybe we could invite him to have dinner with us tomorrow night?" she added hopefully.

Lee studied the expression on Sam's face. *Why was she so anxious to see Donovan again?* He shrugged. "OK, let me send him a text."

A couple texts went back and forth between the two. Sam didn't want to seem too overly-anxious. She didn't realize she was chewing on her lip but Lee noticed.

He finally looked up from his phone. "I don't know what this is all about other than you look as nervous as a tic. Donovan said he'd meet us for dinner tomorrow night."

A huge smile crossed Sam's face as her eyes lit up. "Sweet!"

Lee grabbed her hand. "I know you well enough to know you're up to something! Spill it – what's going on?"

Sam almost looked guilty – maybe she shouldn't invite Gabby – but no, there was no harm in inviting both of them to dinner. It's not like they would be going on a *date* or anything, she reasoned.

She took a deep breath, hoping he wouldn't get mad then she blurted out. "I invited Gabby to dinner tomorrow night! I think she and Donovan might really hit it off."

Lee's face clouded over. Before he could say anything she started talking faster. "She just moved down here. She doesn't have any friends. And she's lonely." She added for good measure.

Lee let out a sigh as he looked at her skeptically.

"Don't look at me like that! It's only dinner!" Her eyes begging him to understand and praying he wouldn't say no.

He studied her face thoughtfully. "How can I be upset with you? You're trying to do something good. I just hope it doesn't backfire on you," he warned.

Sam let out a sigh of relief. She just had a feeling about these two. *Just wait and see* she thought.

The girls suddenly appeared and their conversation was interrupted. Bri was looking at her watch. "Mom, we're late. You were supposed to meet us in the lobby 10 minutes ago."

Sam looked sheepishly at her daughter. "I'm sorry, Bri. We were having a conversation and I lost track of time..."

She looked at Lee and sighed, remembering the first part of their conversation about the treasure. "I got a little sidetracked with the dinner plans, but I'd like to talk more later about the other – the plan you and Donovan are working on."

A few minutes later they were standing at the restaurant entrance. The girls quickly glanced around and then pointed to a table nearby. When they reached the table, both boys immediately stood, introduced themselves and shook hands with Sam and Lee. *At least they were starting off on the right foot!*

After a couple minutes of small talk, they all picked a seat and started to sit down. The boys pulled out the chairs for the girls before seating themselves. *So far, so good!*

Lee looked at Sam, eyebrows raised. Yes, these two had definitely passed the initial test.

Dinner was loud and entertaining. For the most part, Sam and Lee sat back, listening to the four of them talk about their adventures so far. They discovered Travis and Luke had steady jobs and promising careers. And, last but not least, both attended a local church regularly. In fact, they volunteered with the youth group in their free time.

Even Brianna and Jasmine were surprised by this bit of information. "You never told us that!"

By the end of the evening, both boys had Lee and Sam's seal of approval. Sam studied her daughter's expression. She'd never seen her so enthralled by a guy. She really, really liked this Travis. *Hmm ... maybe he is the one.*

Sam mused to herself. *Wouldn't that be something if both of us found "Mr. Right" at almost the same time?* Just the thought of it made her smile.

Lee was looking at Sam. She leaned over and whispered. "Just thinking ... after all these years, this might be "the one."

Lee nodded his head in agreement. He was a pretty good judge of character. In his line of work, you had to be. Both of these young men seemed sincere, hard-working and genuinely cared for

Brianna and Jasmine. Before they knew it, the evening was over.

As they stepped out onto the sidewalk, Travis spoke up.

"Mrs. Rite, would it be OK if the girls hung out with us a little while longer tonight? We're going to meet some of our friends at one of the clubs to go dancing."

Sam glanced at her daughter's pleading face. "Yes, of course. But remember, the three of us are in the same hotel room, so please don't make it too late."

Luke smiled. "Absolutely. We'll have them back by 12:30 or so."

As they turned to go, Sam turned back towards the girls. "Brianna and Jasmine, tomorrow is Friday and it's your last full day here in Florida."

Brianna looked down. "Don't remind me." The downcast face didn't last long as she glanced slyly at her mother. "Mom and I have been talking about moving to Florida."

Lee perked up. "Oh really…"

Before her mom could comment, Brianna continued. "Even though we have family in Michigan, there's nothing holding us there and Mom's cancer has been in remission for a few years now."

She turned to Travis. "I'm sure you can recommend some good cancer doctors since you're in the medical field?"

Sam's heart skipped a beat. She furtively looked over at Lee out of the corner of her eye. He was staring at her intently. Sam lowered her eyes and looked down at the ground.

She was going to get around to this conversation with Lee - but not like this. She sighed heavily. There probably never would be the "perfect moment."

Sam finally spoke up. "Actually, I only need to see Oncologists these days. To make sure it doesn't come back," she finished weakly.

It looked like the discussion was over. After they got in the car, Sam turned to Lee. "What do you think?"

"I think those are some really nice boys. I got a good feel from them and I like to believe I'm a pretty accurate judge of character."

Sam nodded her head thoughtfully. "Yes, I think you're right. Can never be too sure but so far, they get the mom seal-of-approval."

Lee started the car and reached over to put it in gear when he changed his mind. Instead, he turned and looked at Sam. "Is there something we need to talk about?"

Sam glanced at Lee and then looked at her folded hands in her lap. "You mean what Brianna mentioned a minute ago?" She motioned towards the restaurant.

Sam began to nervously twist the ring on her finger. She hesitated. "I was going to get around to telling you, I just hadn't found the right moment..."

Lee said nothing. Instead, he put his hand on top of hers and gave it a reassuring squeeze.

She continued. "You probably don't want to hear all about it."

Lee disagreed. "No. You're wrong. I **do** want to hear all about it."

Sam took a deep breath, started to say something and abruptly stopped. She was so afraid this was going to come out all wrong.

At first the words came out haltingly as if it took everything she had just to speak the words.

Lee could tell from the look on her face this was a very painful subject for her. He spoke softly as he said, "take all the time you need."

Sam could hear herself as she talked but it was almost as if it was someone else's voice. She was stumbling over her words, certain that she was not making the least bit of sense. Lee said nothing as he sat there patiently waiting.

Finally, the dam broke and it all came rushing out. It was as if she was in a hurry to finish. To get it all out as quickly as possible.

Lee nodded a few times and squeezed her hand but not once did he interrupt. As he looked at the woman he was falling in love with, all he could feel was concern and overwhelming compassion.

The last words out of her mouth were the most telling. "I think that's why Anthony cheated on me."

Sam's eyes were shining brightly with unshed tears as she looked over at him. Her voice was now a whisper. "I'm damaged goods, Lee. It's OK if you don't want to see me again. I completely understand."

Lee's expression was unreadable. His eyes were dark as he shook his head. "We'll talk about this when we get back to the hotel."

Without saying another word, he put the car in reverse and backed out of the parking space.

The short ride to the hotel was spent in uncomfortable silence. Sam chewed her lip as she started twisting the ring on her finger again.

She thought about trying to say something but what was there to say? She'd spilled it all. Even gave him an out. Whatever he decided to do – she would have to make peace with it.

The hotel parking lot was full and it took them a few minutes of circling to find an open spot. As soon as the car was parked, Lee quickly jumped out of the driver's seat. For a split second, Sam thought he bolted. Just then, the passenger door swung open. Lee reached down and grabbed Sam's hand, pulling her from her seat.

Without saying a word, he shut the door behind her and headed toward the entrance, still holding onto her hand. He made it to the door within seconds. Sam had to practically run to keep up with his pace.

The night clerk nodded in their direction but Lee was so focused on getting to the elevator, he barely glanced at the guy. He punched the elevator button for the 2nd floor. Thank goodness no one was in the elevator when it opened. She glanced at Lee a couple times but his expression never changed from the dark one he had in the car.

Sam freed her hair from the pony tail and nervously ran her fingers through the long strands. This was not looking good! She swallowed hard and opened her mouth to say something. Nothing came out so she quickly shut it.

When the elevator reached their floor, Lee stepped out first. He was still holding onto her and soon they were on a quick trip to Lee's room.

He fished his room key from his pocket and finally spoke. "Normally, I wouldn't be bringing you back to my room, but I think we need some privacy and this is the best I can do."

Once inside, Lee shut the door and switched on a lamp. Sam sheepishly glanced at his face. Yep - the same expression. Hadn't changed one little bit.

He motioned for her to sit on the small sofa next to the bed. As she sat down, Lee started pacing the floor. Back and forth. Back and forth. Not saying a word.

The look on his face told her now would not be a good time to speak up so she kept quiet.

It looked like he would be wearing a nice spot in the carpet when he abruptly stopped, turned to Sam and said, "Stay right here. Don't move. I'll be back."

With that, he opened the slider door that led out to the balcony. He slowly closed the door and stepped out of sight.

Lee walked to the edge of the balcony, put both hands on the railing and stared straight out at absolutely nothing. He took a deep breath and shut his eyes. The second they were closed, Annie's face appeared. There were days it seemed so long ago – where she was nothing but a distant memory. And there were moments when the pain came rushing back, like a jagged knife stabbing him in the chest. He shook his head and opened his eyes. Was he really ready for this? To love someone and take a chance that once again, they would be taken away by this cruel, unforgiving disease ...

By now, Sam was really starting to worry. Tears welled up in her eyes and threatened to spill over without warning. *This is going even worse than I thought. Maybe I should've just ended it.*

Sam glanced at the clock on the nightstand. Five minutes. Ten minutes. It seemed like an eternity before the slider door opened. Sam looked up. The expression on his face wasn't that dark, brooding stare. Instead, his look was very thoughtful – and very sad.

He walked over, sat down beside Sam and reached for her hand. He didn't waste any time before he started to speak. "My wife, Annie, died of cancer. Pancreatic cancer."

He had a catch in his voice as he continued. "Sam, it was a horrible death. To lose someone you love, someone I loved as much as I did Annie, to cancer - was almost unbearable."

He unconsciously squeezed her hand as he continued. "I swore I would never love again – or at least never love someone as much as I loved Annie and open myself up to that kind of pain."

He turned and looked directly into Sam's eyes. "Until now. Until I met you."

The look on Lee's face was one of almost unbearable pain. "When Brianna said you had cancer back there in the restaurant, I felt like the floor had dropped out from underneath me. Again."

"My mind was reeling. Sam, I've grown to love you and everything about you. I just can't imagine my life without you in it."

He looked up, as if searching for the right words to say. "I know we haven't known each other for a long time, but we've been through a lot together and I feel that it's time for me to start living again. To start loving again."

He nodded towards the balcony. "When I was out there, I was thinking. What would Annie want for me?" He grabbed both of her hands, giving them a gentle squeeze. "Annie would want this for me. She would want me to be happy. And she would love you."

He took a deep breath. "Crazy as this may sound, maybe this is a sign – that you are the one."

Lee cupped his hand under Sam's chin as he looked into her eyes. "I'm glad I know now. You are a beautiful, spirited, gentle soul and I love you."

Sam blinked. She was at a loss for words. Huge tears slowly started rolling down her cheeks.

As Lee wrapped his arms around her, holding her tight, Sam began sobbing uncontrollably. Heart wrenching sobs shook her body as the pent-up pain and grief of feeling unloved for so long was unleashed.

The tighter Lee held her, the harder she cried.

After every single tear had been cried and every ounce of pain had surfaced, Sam finally pulled herself together and lifted her head.

"I'm sorry, I don't normally break down like that, I just..."

He put a finger to her lips, "Shhh..."

His hand gently caressed her face as he leaned forward to kiss her ever-so-softly. It took Sam's breath away. It was sweet, gentle and loving, all at once.

Lee pulled away and looked down at her – a look of pure adoration for the woman he loved.

Sam wiped the back of her hand across her tear stained face. "I'm sure I'm a sight right now."

Lee nodded. "A beautiful one at that."

"I need a minute to pull myself together ... if you don't mind?" She headed towards the bathroom.

She flipped on the light and peered into the mirror. It was worse than she thought. Her face was splotchy. Her eyes bloodshot and her nose bright red. There were long, black mascara streaks running down her cheeks.

She splashed cold water on her face and did her best to wipe away the black lines the mascara left behind. Moments later, she returned to where Lee was still sitting.

"There's my gorgeous lady!"

Sam gave him a watery smile. "Don't lie to me!"

"No lie. I think you're the prettiest woman on the planet."

They sat and talked for a long time. Lee wanted to make sure Sam felt secure in the fact that he loved her – and he wasn't going anywhere! He would be right there, no matter what.

Finally, it was time for Sam to head back to her room. When they reached her door, Lee swiftly pulled her into his arms. She tipped her head back, waiting for his glorious kiss. She didn't have to wait long. His lips possessed hers, as if he couldn't own them completely enough.

Without hesitation, Sam returned the intensity. She belonged to Lee! He knew everything and he still wanted her! It sent a thrilling tingle down her spine.

The pair were oblivious to their surroundings when suddenly right behind them a throat cleared, "Ahem!" They pulled away guiltily. Jasmine and Brianna were standing behind them.

"I thought we better break you two up. It looked like we could be waiting here awhile."

Lee laughed. "Well, I guess that'll teach us."

He turned back to Sam. "I have some work to wrap up tomorrow morning. I'll be house-hunting in the afternoon." He continued. "Looks like they're going to approve my transfer so I'll be moving down here in the next month or so."

Brianna cut him off, "You're MOVING here?" She turned to her mom. "He's moving here. Mom, this is a sign!"

Brianna was just about beside herself. "OK, that settles it. We need to start looking for a house, too!"

Lee and Sam started laughing at the same time. "Brianna, it's not that easy..."

She wasn't going to take no for an answer. "... but checking the area out might not be a bad idea."

"Yes!" Bri turned to look at Jasmine.

She shrugged. "I'm in, too. I love it down here! My mom will be less-than-thrilled but she can always come visit. Or move here, too!" she added.

Lee looked at his watch. "House hunting in the afternoon, it is. I'll meet you ladies in the lobby around 2."

With that, they said good-night and headed inside.

Chapter 14

Another day of glorious sunshine greeted them the next morning. Since the girls were leaving soon, they wanted to finish up some last-minute shopping.

Sam let them go off by themselves as she settled into the hotel room. She needed to catch up on some office work while it was quiet.

The morning was gone before she knew it. Soon, they were in the lobby, waiting for Lee to pick them up.

House-hunting was fun and Sam was surprised at how much she liked all four houses they looked at. The homes were in really nice neighborhoods. The streets were lined with broad sidewalks and huge oak trees and almost all lawns meticulously manicured.   Everything looked so green and lush. She loved the tropical-feel that just seemed to pour out of everything. Palm trees were everywhere.   Although the style of the homes were quite different than what she was used to in

Michigan, it was something she could definitely get used to, she thought to herself.

"Mom, we need to have palm trees in *our* yard!" Brianna exclaimed.

The girls liked all the houses, but their favorites were definitely the ones with in-ground pools. Sam had to admit she liked the idea of having a pool, too. A couple of them had what they called screened lanais. The realtor explained this was to keep bugs and pesky critters out. And, he pointed out, there was less maintenance if the pools were screened in.

Hmmm, that made sense to Sam. Guess we'll need a screen if we get a pool. The dollar signs were adding up.

Lee's favorite was a pool home that backed up to a golf course.

"Good choice." The realtor confirmed. "Better for resale value. Golf course homes are very popular down here."

Lee turned to Sam. "Do you golf?"

Bri snorted. "No, but I'd sure like to see her try."

"Brianna, that's not nice!" Sam scolded.

She wrinkled up her nose and turned back to Lee. "For you, I would try it."

Lee thanked the realtor and said he would get back with him in the next day or two, after he had a chance to talk it over with Sam. When they got back in the car, Lee asked her what she thought.

She agreed the golf course pool home was her favorite but reminded him that she wasn't the one buying it. "Maybe not, but you may be living in it one day - soon." He matter-of-factly stated.

Brianna leaned over the front seat. "Wow, you two are getting serious." For once, Sam was at a loss for words. She was right. It was getting serious – more serious by the minute.

When it was time for Lee and Sam to meet Donovan and Gabby for dinner, they left the girls out on the pool deck to enjoy their last night in Florida and spend some time with Luke and Travis.

On the ride to the restaurant, Sam was getting butterflies and having second thoughts about Donovan and Gabby meeting. *What if they can't stand each other? Or, what if they do like each other, something happens and they stopped dating and then blamed Sam?*

Lee looked over at Sam and chuckled. "Maybe it wasn't such a great idea having them meet, after all?"

Sam slapped Lee's arm. "Stop it. Just getting cold feet for them, I guess," she admitted.

She'd find out soon enough. When they arrived at the restaurant, they asked for a table outside, in the corner so they could keep an eye out.

Donovan arrived first. He didn't seem the least bit concerned about an extra dinner guest as he reached over to give Sam a gentle hug and slap Lee on the back. It didn't really matter if Donovan was nervous – Sam was nervous enough for both of them.

When they sat down, she decided maybe it was best to describe Gabby a little – give him a bit of a warning about her over-the-top-personality. But how could she put it in a way that wouldn't scare him half-to-death?

She opened her mouth to speak but it was too late! Before she had a chance to give Donovan the lowdown, she spotted Gabby as she stepped onto the sidewalk in front of the restaurant. Sam slapped her hand to her forehead. *What on earth did that woman have on?*

Lee followed her gaze. "Well, will you look at that?" He smirked as he looked over at Sam. "This ought to be interesting!"

To say Gabby was all decked out would be a major understatement. She was wearing a little black dress with a deep slit up the side. It was skin-tight with a plunging V-neck that accentuated her ample bosom. She was wearing a huge, gold necklace. The shiny, round discs did nothing to hide Gabby's – ahem – "assets." A crimson red, rhinestone-studded belt was cinched tightly around her waist. It would have looked seriously out of place if not for the 6-inch vibrant red stiletto heels she had strapped on her feet. Sam could hear Gabby clanking as she wobbled down the sidewalk. By the looks of it, she had enough gold bracelets on to open her own jewelry store!

As if that wasn't enough, she was smacking her gum as she talked loudly into her cell phone. You could hear every word coming out of her mouth. "Donna, I'm telling you, this isn't gonna work. You can't just up and quitcher' job and move down here. I mean you need money. M-O-N-E-Y!!"

Just then she glanced around. She had an audience. "Look, I gotta go. I'm meetin' friends for dinner. I think they got a hot one for me – if ya' know what I mean."

Seconds later, she spotted Lee and Sam sitting at the table and waved a clanking arm in their direction. "Heyyyy!! YooHoo!! OVER HERE!!!"

She put the phone close to her mouth and continued the conversation. "Look, I gotta run!" She tried to lower her voice and whisper to "Donna" on the other end but it didn't work. You could still hear every word she said. "He's *gorgeous*. Look, I'll call ya' later. Bye!"

With that, she snapped her phone shut and ran a hand through her unruly red locks. Still chomping away on the gum, she must've decided now was the time to ditch it. She craned her head as she scoped out the nicely-landscaped bushes and colorful spring flowers surrounding the deck. She bent over, her ample chest threatening to blow out the sides and "patoop." The gum was clearly no longer a problem.

By now, most of the other diners were staring at Gabby – including Donovan. Sam sneaked a furtive peek at him as she tried to gauge his reaction. Stone-faced. She had no idea what was going through his mind.

Sam nervously wiped a hand across her brow as she swallowed hard.

Lee looked over at her. By the look on his face, she could tell he was **thoroughly** enjoying her discomfort.

There was nothing left to do except walk over and say hello to her friend. *Friend?* Well, maybe that wasn't quite an accurate description. More like an acquaintance...

Gabby spotted Sam as she stood and picked up her wobbly pace. She seemed so excited to see her, Sam felt guilty about being so judgmental.

The guys stood just as they reached the table. Lee spoke first. "Gabby, this is my friend Donovan. Donovan, this is Gabby, our friend from the cruise."

Donovan quickly offered his hand. Instead of shaking it like a normal person would, Gabby grabbed his hand and turned it over. "Such nice, strong hands! OOHHH, look at that – you have some interesting lines... For instance, look at your heart line..."

Sam snatched Donovan's hand away from Gabby. "We will not be doing any palm reading. That's pure witchcraft."

Gabby's face fell. "I'm sorry, I just..."

Sam felt bad. She may have overreacted just a tad but this was no way to leave a first impression. Instead, she quickly changed the subject.

"Let's just sit down." She glanced around. "We're getting a lot of unwanted attention. Well, maybe not for you, but at least for me it's unwanted."

Lee could see Sam struggling. He sighed as he saved her once again. "Gabby, you look delightful. I forgot how very interesting and entertaining you really are."

Sam looked suspiciously at Lee. *Was he serious?*

Gabby brightened at the compliment as she reached up and patted her bright red locks. "Thanks. And I forgot how absolutely gorgeous you are." She paused and then looked at Donovan. "But not *nearly* as gorgeous as your friend here."

With that, Gabby monopolized the entire conversation. She was talking when they ordered appetizers. She talked non-stop while they ate their meal. She was STILL talking when they ordered coffee and dessert.

Sam was slightly annoyed until she reminded herself that this dinner was all about Gabby and Donovan meeting each other.

She sneaked a look at Donovan. It was hard to tell what he was thinking. He didn't look like he was put-off or if he was, he was doing a good job of hiding it. Sam sent up a small prayer of thanks that the whole thing hadn't blown up in her face.

She glanced at Lee. He was extremely amused and didn't seem the least bit bothered by Gabby's unending chatter.

Finally, much to Sam's relief, the evening ended and it was time to go. Donovan quickly stood up and ran over to pull Gabby's chair out for her.

Sam's mouth dropped open. *Well, I'll be darned. I think he really likes her!*

She looked over at Lee who had the same look of surprise on his face. She smiled smugly and Lee returned the look with a shake of his head as if to say, *I really can't believe this.*

The four of them walked to where Gabby's car was parked. Donovan turned to Gabby, acting as if Sam and Lee were invisible. He reached out and squeezed Gabby's hand. "I would love to have dinner with you again."

He fished a card from his wallet and handed it to her. "Here's my work card. My cell number is on it. Give me a call after you get home later and we'll figure out when we can meet for dinner again."

With that, he reached over and gently kissed Gabby's cheek. She must have been just as shocked as Sam because her mouth dropped open and for once, she was at a loss for words. She just nodded her head.

Finally, she squeaked out. "Sam, thanks so much for asking me to dinner." She looked back at Donovan. "I had the best time *ever.*"

Sam raised her eyebrows as she looked over at Lee triumphantly. *See, I told you!*

Lee just shook his head as Gabby drove off. When they got to Donovan's car, Lee turned to his friend. "You don't have to go out with her again, you know."

Donovan looked puzzled. "But why not? I thought she was absolutely enchanting. Like a breath of fresh air." He looked back to where Gabby had just pulled out and smiled. "She reminds me of home."

With that, he jumped in his car. Just before he backed out, he rolled down the window. "We need to get together soon to talk about that diving trip."

Sam had almost forgotten about that! Ugh, now something else for her to have to worry about!

Sam and Lee headed to their car. As soon as the doors shut, Sam opened her mouth to say something but Lee held up his hand to stop her. "You don't have to say a word. You were right – I was wrong." A look of amazement crossed his face. "Still, I never would've put those two together..."

Sam crossed her arms and tilted her head to the side triumphantly. "That's because you're a guy and you know nothing about women's intuition!"

With that, Lee shook his head and laughed. "You got that right! Nor do I want to!"

When they got back to the hotel, they headed out to the pool deck to see if the kids were still outside. Sam spied them at a corner table under the lights. Just then Brianna spotted her mom and waved them over.

All four of them looked glum. "Why all the sad faces? It's not like you'll never see each other ever again..."

Brianna looked at her mom pleadingly. "Honestly, mom. Are you *really* going to consider moving to Florida?"

Sam sighed as she glanced around the table and then back at Lee. Now it was five glum faces staring at her. She was definitely outnumbered. "Yes, I think we should give it some serious consideration." She had to admit that she liked what she'd seen today and that getting a job transfer would be fairly easy. The more she thought about it, the more sense it seemed to make.

Brianna's face lit up. Sam put her hands on her hips. "But ... it's not like we can up and move tomorrow. It's going to take planning and more research," she warned.

She looked over at her daughter, a serious expression on her face. "The first thing we're going to do is pray about it. We're not moving anywhere without seeking God's direction on this."

Brianna ignored the second part of what her mom said as she jumped up and ran over to throw her arms around her neck. "You are the BEST Mom in the whole world and I love you!"

Sam hugged her back as she tried to reason with her. "Remember Bri – it's not going to happen overnight."

Just then Lee walked over and placed his hand on Sam's back. "I'll help in any way I can, even if I have to fly to Michigan, rent a truck and move you down here myself."

Before he could finish his sentence, the boys chimed in. "We'll help, too. We can drive up there and help you move!"

Jasmine sat there with her head in her hands, not saying a word. She was the only one still looking unhappy. Sam walked over and sat down beside her. She put her arm around Jasmine's shoulder and softly said, "Jasmine, I know what you're thinking. That we're all going to move down here and you'll be left in Michigan all alone. But remember, your mom, your family – they're all up there. This is a big decision – that only you can make."

She looked over at Bri. "I'm sure Brianna would love for you to move here, too. Just remember, no one can make that decision for you. So go home. Think about it – and I mean *really* think about it."

Jasmine looked over at Sam with tear-filled eyes. "I know you're right, Mrs. Rite." She paused as she looked over at Luke. "And I promise I will give it some serious thought."

Sam squeezed her hand reassuringly as she stood back up. "It's getting late. We better head up. The girls have to be at the airport pretty early tomorrow."

She looked at Brianna. "I'll give you a few minutes to say your good-byes and then I'll see you back in the room."

When they reached the girls' hotel room. Sam stopped and looked at Lee expectantly. "I think you owe me something."

Lee looked down at her, his eyes smiling. "Yes, I believe I do."

With that, he reached over and gently pushed Sam's long silky strands away from her face, their eyes locking. Without hesitation, Sam reached up and put her arms around Lee's neck as his arms reached out and pulled her to him.

When his lips touched hers, it was the sweetest kiss Sam had ever experienced. Her heart pounded as all the love and tenderness she felt for him was wrapped up in the gentleness of her emotions. The kiss deepened as Sam let out a long sigh. She wished this kiss could last forever.

Finally, Lee pulled back, a small smile playing on his lips. "We better stop now. If not, the girls will catch us again and they'll think all we ever do is stand outside your door and make out."

Sam let out a small giggle and sighed again. "Yeah, you're right. I guess it's a good thing they're here. We don't want to get carried away ... or, do we?"

She didn't give him time to answer before she stuck the key card in the door and opened it up.

"I'll need to take them to the airport in the morning. That leaves me one more day before I have to go back..."

Lee shoved his hands in his pockets and frowned. "Don't remind me. Soon, I'll be just as miserable as the group we just left."

He continued. "That'll just motivate me to get you down here as quickly as possible!"

With that, he reached over and planted a quick kiss on Sam's cheek before turning to go.

Chapter 15

The next morning the skies were overcast and gloomy, which matched the girls' moods perfectly. They were down-in-the-dumps over having to leave Travis and Luke. Sam tried to cheer them up to no avail. They didn't even want to eat breakfast.

At the airport, Sam was feeling a little guilty that she was staying on with Lee and the girls had to leave. But it had to be done and soon, they were on their way into the terminal. Sam let out a huge sigh of relief as she watched them go.

On the trip back to the hotel, she was glad for a few minutes to herself. So much had happened in the last several days, it was nice to just be alone. She spent time every morning in quiet prayer but there were moments she just needed more than that.

Her alone-time with God was the most important part of her day. Even though she knew He was in every situation and every moment of her life, it just felt good to talk out loud to Him. With every fiber of her being, she knew He was listening and that He loved her more than she could possibly comprehend. She ended her time with Him in earnest prayer.

"Dear God. Thank you for loving me. Thank you for forgiving me of all my sins. I cherish my alone-time with You and as I pour out my heart, I feel Your presence so close to me.

Thank you, Jesus, for dying for me, for cleansing me of all my sins now and forever. Lead me as you would have me go today, tomorrow and always. In Jesus precious name, I pray. Amen."

Just that small amount of time Sam had in the car made all the difference in her soul and in her mind.

She had the rest of the day to herself since she wasn't going to meet Lee until later in the afternoon. She almost felt guilty about being so happy to have time alone.

The afternoon flew by as she worked on her computer in the hotel room. She finally glanced at her watch. She needed to get ready – Lee would be back soon!

With that, she hopped out of her chair and rushed to the bathroom. She wanted to spend extra time getting ready since this was their last evening until who-knew-when.

She had just finished putting her hair up in a sleek, smooth updo when she heard a knock on the door. She ran over and quickly opened it to find Lee standing there and he was all decked out. "Wow! Look at you all dressed up! What's the special occasion?"

"Since this is our last night, I wanted it to be special. It's a surprise."

She was intrigued. With that, she grabbed her handbag and followed him down the hall. No matter how much Sam tried to wheedle it out of him, he just shook his head adamantly. The only things she knew were that they were driving away from Orlando and toward the ocean.

Eventually, they pulled into a parking lot in what seemed like the middle of nowhere. Sam looked around. There were lots of cars but when she looked at the building, it was anything but exciting. In fact, you couldn't see much of the building at all. There were huge oak trees dotting the lawn. They were covered with huge clumps of hanging moss. The trees and hanging moss cast an eerie shadow over the building. Sam shivered involuntarily. "Where did you bring me – to a haunted restaurant?"

He shook his head emphatically. "No, this place came highly recommended. Just wait."

Sam glanced at the large bronze plaque hanging at the entrance into the restaurant. *Breakers by the Sea.*

He was right. When they got inside, Sam was in awe. The place was absolutely stunning. The view from the front entrance was amazing. Beautifully decorated and elegant candle-lit tables filled the room. Every table had an expansive ocean view. Leaded glass windows and French doors separated the dining room from a long, wooden porch. The porch was filled with white wicker potted plants and padded antique rocking chairs. Wrought iron lamp posts adorned the railing and cast a romantic evening glow.

Sam turned to Lee, her eyes shining. "This place is just perfect."

With that, they were quickly seated at a table for two by the window. Sam couldn't get enough of the amazing view. She thought the place was absolutely heavenly until she glanced at the menu. The place was definitely not cheap. Lee must've realized what she was thinking. "Please order whatever you like. This is our last evening alone and I want it to be special."

The menu wasn't huge but there was a tempting variety. She settled on the five-cheese baked lasagna with a small garden salad, relieved that she was able to find something that wasn't too awful expensive.

Lee ordered the baked fish with garlic mashed potatoes and steamed broccoli.

The meal was wonderful, the atmosphere cozy and very romantic. They shared each other's dinner and both proclaimed the other's to be much better. After the waiter brought the coffee out, Lee leaned back in his chair. "So Donovan and I have plans to search for the sunken treasure soon."

Sam set her coffee cup down as she carefully picked her words. She didn't want to discourage his dreams of treasure, but she knew there were others who also saw the map and would more-than-likely be searching for it, too. Some really bad people.

"I know I can't talk you out of this – and maybe I don't really want to," she admitted. "But will you promise me that you'll be really, really careful and not do anything crazy?"

Lee leaned forward. "Yes, of course. I'm not naïve enough to think that Beth and Tom didn't get a copy – or Michel or possibly even others."

"I think we have just as good a chance of finding it as they do – maybe even better!"

Sam felt a knot tighten in her stomach. She shook her head. "I'll be praying for you – daily – and you need to let me know exactly when you'll be going out to search for it."

Lee promised he would. He could see how visibly upset this was making her, so he quickly changed the subject.

Soon, it was time to go. Sam looked around one more time when they reached the door. This was such a beautiful place. Maybe someday he would bring her here again.

The ride back to the hotel was quiet. Sam could relate to the sadness the girls felt the night before, knowing they were leaving someone they cared for behind.

Sensing her mood, Lee reached over and grabbed her hand and gave it a gentle squeeze. "I hope this motivates you to get a move on – literally!"

She slowly nodded. "I think it will."

Back at her hotel room, she turned to Lee. "I think it will be too painful saying good-bye tomorrow, so maybe I should just take a taxi to the airport."

Lee didn't answer right away as he studied her face. Finally, he nodded. "You're probably right."

With that, she stood on her tippy-toes as she leaned in and pulled him towards her. Her kiss was a promise. A promise that she would see him soon. She couldn't bear to say "good-bye." Instead, she gave him a small, shaky smile before she turned and walked into her room, closing the door firmly behind her.

The end.

The Story Continues...Download Book 3 (Tides of Deception) At HopeCallaghan.com

Visit my website for new releases and special offers: hopecallaghan.com

About The Author

Hope Callaghan is an author who loves to write Christian books, especially Christian Mystery and Cozy Mystery books. Born and raised in a small town in West Michigan, she now lives in Florida with her husband.

She is the proud mother of one daughter and a stepdaughter and stepson. When she's not doing the thing she loves best - writing books - she enjoys cooking, traveling and reading books.

Hope loves to connect with her readers!

Visit **hopecallaghan.com** for information on special offers and soon-to-be-released books!

Email: hope@hopecallaghan.com

Facebook page:
http://www.facebook.com/hopecallaghanauthor

Other Books by Author, Hope Callaghan:

DECEPTION CHRISTIAN MYSTERY SERIES:

Waves of Deception: Samantha Rite Series Book 1
Winds of Deception: Samantha Rite Series Book 2
Tides of Deception: Samantha Rite Series Book 3

GARDEN GIRLS CHRISTIAN COZY MYSTERIES SERIES:

Who Murdered Mr. Malone? Garden Girls Mystery Series Book 1
Grandkids Gone Wild: Garden Girls Mystery Series Book 2
Smoky Mountain Mystery: Garden Girls Mystery Series Book 3
Death by Dumplings: Garden Girls Mystery Series Book 4
Eye Spy: Garden Girls Mystery Series Book 5
Magnolia Mansion Mysteries: Garden Girls Mystery Series Book 6
Missing Milt: Garden Girls Mystery Series Book 7
Book 8 Coming Soon!

CRUISE SHIP CHRISTIAN COZY MYSTERIES SERIES:

Starboard Secrets: Cruise Ship Cozy Mysteries Book 1
Portside Peril: Cruise Ship Cozy Mysteries Book 2
Lethal Lobster: Cruise Ship Cozy Mysteries Book 3

Visit my website for new releases and special offers: hopecallaghan.com

Preview Book 3(Tides of Deception)

Tides of Deception

Samantha Rite Series Book 3

Hope Callaghan

Visit my website for new releases and special offers: hopecallaghan.com

FIRST EDITION

hopecallaghan.com

But lay up for yourselves treasures in heaven, where neither moth nor rust doth corrupt, and where thieves do not break through nor steal. For where your treasure is, there will your heart be also.
Matthew 6:20-21. KJV

Lee adjusted the dive mask on his face. He nodded his head and gave the thumbs up just before he fell backward, out of the small boat and into the deep blue water. He knew the exact direction he needed to take as he forced the fins on his feet to move faster.

There wasn't much daylight left and he wasn't keen on being out in open water when night fell. With the passing of Hurricane Bartholomew, the seas were still a bit rough, their chances of discovering the treasure were getting slimmer and slimmer every day.

Within minutes, Lee reached the spot he'd been looking for. The rock shelf was long and bumpy.

In the distance, he could see where it raised up. *Yes! This was it.* His heart started thumping hard as he pushed himself down past the peak of the shelf.

He pulled his dive light out of its protective pouch and quickly turned it on. Now that the whole shelf was illuminated, he pointed it downward. Nothing. He pulled himself just a few inches lower. He didn't want to go too far down. Without the right gear it was dangerous to have that much pressure on his body and the equipment.

He carefully studied the area illuminated by the bright light. At first he saw only deep blue water. He was just about to give up when something caught his eye. Something shiny. Yes, there was definitely something directly below him. With his free hand, he pulled the folding stick out of the storage pouch that was attached to his buoyancy controller. He quickly opened it up and began poking around near the shiny object, careful not to stir up too much sediment or else he wouldn't be able to see anything. The stick hit on something hard. As he slid it sideways, he could see more shiny objects. He pulled the stick back up and carefully hooked a small net onto the end. Once more, he pushed the stick down into the murky bottom. Ever-so-gently he scooped up one of the shiny objects.

He took a deep breath as he slowly brought the net up for a closer inspection. *Crap!* He was so nervous and excited, his heavy breathing was making his mask fog up! There was just one small clear spot so he wiggled it around to get the best close up view possible. He shined his flashlight directly on the object as he peered at it from the edge of his mask. His eyes grew wide when he saw what he'd been looking for all this time. It was a Spanish cob coin with a cross etched on the center. It was faint but it was definitely there!

Lee's mind was racing – they found it – they finally found it!!! He folded the diving stick and carefully placed that and the coin inside the zippered compartment and securely zipped it.

He started his ascent back to the surface when he suddenly remembered. *What an idiot! This was the most important part of the dive!* He reached into another pouch on the other side of his buoyancy controller and pulled out his underwater GPS. With the location coordinates safely stored inside, Lee started his slow ascent to the top where Donovan was anxiously waiting.

Donovan peered over the edge of the boat into the murky water. He was starting to get nervous. Lee had been down there a long time – longer than normal. His sharp eyes keeping a lookout for the tiny bubbles letting him know Lee was coming up. He was so focused on figuring out if Lee was alright that he didn't hear the approaching boat.

Donovan started to lose his balance. Something just hit the side of the boat! He grabbed the edge to steady himself as he looked back to see what caused the commotion.

Another, larger boat had pulled up beside him and there were two strange men inside. He was just about to ask them what the heck they were doing when one of them jumped into his boat and rushed towards him.

There was no time to react – it was all happening so quickly! The stranger was now standing over him, a gun in his hand, pointed right at Donovan's head.

Just then he noticed bubbles rising from the water next to the boat. Lee was surfacing! The gunman noticed too. Seconds later Lee popped out of the water. He was so excited he spit his mouthpiece out and practically shouted at Donovan. "I found it, I mean WE found it – we found the treasure!"

Just then he spotted the man standing next to Donovan, holding a gun. The gunman was grinning from ear-to-ear. "That's the best news I've heard all day!"

The Story Continues…Download Book 3 (Tides of Deception) At <u>HopeCallaghan.com</u>

Visit my website for new releases and special offers: <u>hopecallaghan.com</u>

Made in the USA
Monee, IL
06 March 2021